Praise for *Cape*

"*Cape* is a book with something for everyone—codes to crack, villains to vanquish, and a trio of superheroes who just might save the world. An absolutely original story, filled with so much excitement that the pages practically turn themselves."

—FRANCES O'ROARK DOWELL,
Edgar Award–winning author of *Dovey Coe*

"A one-two punch of heroism and fun!"

—INGRID LAW,
Newbery Honor winner and *New York Times* bestselling author of *Savvy*

"Josie, Mae, and Akiko aren't just the friends and superheroes we need today, they're the friends and superheroes we need to *be* today. These girls rock!"

—LIESL SHURTLIFF,
New York Times bestselling author of the Time Castaways trilogy

"Kate Hannigan does more than write a rip-roaring girls' adventure story. She brings back to life real women who were real superheroines . . . along with some sadly forgotten but wonderful fictional superheroines who predated Wonder Woman. I can't wait for Book Two!"

—TRINA ROBBINS,
author of *Babes in Arms, Women in Comics During the Second World War*

★"Readers across genres will be enamored by this blend of history, mystery, and superpowered action."

—*BOOKLIST* starred review

"Fans of fast-paced action adventures, computer science, and confident main characters will enjoy this series debut that is sure to fly off the shelves."

—*SLJ*

"With interwoven action sequences told in comics panels, the tale has the exciting pace of a superhero adventure. Puzzles readers can solve are the icing on this cake."

—*KIRKUS REVIEWS*

Praise for *Mask*

"A winning blend of comedy, superheroics, inspirational women from history, and puzzle-solving."

—*KIRKUS REVIEWS*

Don't miss the other adventures in
THE LEAGUE OF SECRET HEROES series!

Cape

Mask

THE LEAGUE OF SECRET HEROES

Boots

Book Three

WITHDRAWN

By KATE HANNIGAN

Illustrated by PATRICK SPAZIANTE

Aladdin

New York London Toronto Sydney New Delhi

ALADDIN
An imprint of Simon & Schuster Children's Publishing Division
1230 Avenue of the Americas, New York, New York 10020
First Aladdin hardcover edition August 2021
Text copyright © 2021 by Kate Hannigan
Jacket illustrations copyright © 2021 by Elan Harris
Interior illustrations copyright © 2021 by Patrick Spaziante
All rights reserved, including the right of reproduction in whole or in part in any form.
ALADDIN and related logo are registered trademarks of Simon & Schuster, Inc.
For information about special discounts for bulk purchases, please contact Simon & Schuster Special Sales at 1-866-506-1949 or business@simonandschuster.com.
The Simon & Schuster Speakers Bureau can bring authors to your live event. For more information or to book an event contact the Simon & Schuster Speakers Bureau at 1-866-248-3049 or visit our website at www.simonspeakers.com.
Jacket designed by Laura Lyn DiSiena
Interior designed by Tom Daly
The illustrations for this book were rendered digitally.
The text of this book was set in Marion.
Manufactured in the United States of America 0621 FFG
2 4 6 8 10 9 7 5 3 1
Library of Congress Cataloging-in-Publication Data
Names: Hannigan, Kate, author. | Spaziante, Patrick, illustrator. | Title: Boots / by Kate Hannigan ; illustrated by Patrick Spaziante. | Description: First Aladdin hardcover edition. | New York : Aladdin, 2021. | Series: The League of Secret Heroes ; 3 | Audience: Ages 8-12. | Summary: When Mae's Aunt Willa and Aunt Janet, both pilots, are kidnapped by evil Metallic Falcon, Josie, Mae, and Akiko, the Infinity Trinity, pursue them from Chicago to Sweetwater, Texas, to Paris, France.
Identifiers: LCCN 2020050400 (print) | LCCN 2020050401 (ebook) | ISBN 9781534439177 (hardcover) | ISBN 9781534439191 (ebook) |
Subjects: CYAC: Superheroes—Fiction. | Spies—Fiction. | Kidnapping—Fiction. | Women air pilots—Fiction. | Pilots—Fiction. | African Americans—Fiction. | Chicago (Ill.)—History—20th century—Fiction. | Paris (France)—History—1940-1944—Fiction. | France—History—German occupation, 1940-1945—Fiction.
Classification: LCC PZ7.H198158 Boo 2021 (print) | LCC PZ7.H198158 (ebook) | DDC [Fic]—dc23
LC record available at https://lccn.loc.gov/2020050400

For Jenni Braun & Joey Journeycake,
my original Infinity Trinity

Boots

These planes remind me of Nova the Sunchaser.

Her plane has a force field to protect her.

NOVA THE SUNCHASER SOARS

I wish ALL these planes had Nova's force field.

What scares you about flying, Mae?

Heights?

As the Violet Vortex, it's no problem . . .

: . . . but as regular old me, I'm scared to make a MISTAKE.

Two

BRAVERY ISN'T ABOUT BATTLING BACK SUPER-villains. Most of the time, being brave means looking at the things that scare us and pushing past them.

Like spiders. Or thunderstorms. Or making a mistake.

"Mae Eugenia Crumpler!" came a shout. "What in the world are you doing here in Chicago, Illinois? Did you run away from that summer camp?"

At the sight of what must have been her granny, Mae's eyebrows shot so high, they could have bumped a bird passing overhead. And her mouth started moving, but no sound came out. I gave a jump too. Not only because the sudden appearance of a little old lady yelling at us was surprising. But also because that little old lady looked so tiny and fragile and, well, sweet.

She seemed like somebody who'd serve us a plate of warm cookies. Not yell at us like a drill sergeant in the army.

Mae's granny peered over her horn-rimmed glasses, eyes ablaze.

"What do you have to say for yourself, Mae Eugenia?" she said, waving a knobby finger in our direction.

How could we explain where we'd been all this time? And even if we did explain it—that we'd fought off a supervillain called Side-Splitter and his army of evil clowns, that we'd saved innocent people and maybe even the whole city of San Francisco from Side-Splitter's destruction, that we'd helped catch a spy who was sending secret messages to the Japanese military, and that we'd discovered Akiko's mom was working to beat the Nazis with Room Twelve, too, just like us—Granny Crumpler wouldn't believe it.

I barely could myself.

"Anybody want a candy bar?" asked Akiko, clearly trying to divert attention from speechless Mae. She pulled a few bars from her Hauntima bag and passed them around. "These are delicious," she said, holding out the sweets toward Mae's grandmother. "I picked them up from this chocolate shop out in San Fra—"

"Santa's Village!" I interrupted, taking a half step in front of Akiko.

She was going to spill the beans that we'd been out in San Francisco! When we were supposed to be at a sleep-away camp somewhere in the woods near Philadelphia! I shot her the stink-eye.

"Santa's Village?" asked Granny Crumpler. "Where's that?"

"Right," Akiko said, finally catching on. She shoved the last chocolate bar back into her bag. "Um. Santa's Village. It's . . . *umm* . . . north. Of . . . Philadelphia."

I wanted to smack my forehead. This was not going well.

"Mae Eugenia, I received word from Mrs.-what's-her-name. Mrs. Bow, Mrs. Bah—"

"Mrs. Boudica," Mae said, finally able to speak. "We call her Mrs. B."

My breath caught in my throat. Constance Boudica was one of the heads of Room Twelve. She needed us to find her sister, Dolores, who was better known as the remarkable Zenobia. And not just find her, but bring Zenobia—and all the other missing superheroes—back home.

"Mrs. Boudica said you girls would be gone most of the summer at that overnight camp," continued Granny Crumpler. "Is she a librarian or a principal, this Mrs. B? I believe she works at your friend Josephine's school? Which of you is Josephine?"

Now it was my turn to squirm under Granny Crumpler's intense gaze.

"I'm J-Josie," I stammered. "She's a—a good teacher."

I did not want to lie to Granny Crumpler. But I was not going to be the one to slip up and reveal our other identity—as the superhero trio Infinity Trinity.

"Yes," agreed Mae, nodding a little too enthusiastically. "Mrs. B's teaching us so many important things."

"Math skills, scientific discovery, language arts," added Akiko. But then she couldn't stop. "Self-defense, military strategy—"

I bumped her with my hip to tone it down. Granny Crumpler seemed like the type who could sniff out a lie.

"I just arrived on the train from Philadelphia a couple of days ago," Granny began. "I opened the new library branch there, and I have to go back soon. But I wanted to check on Willa and Janet, make sure things are all right here at home."

Aunt Willa and Aunt Janet, who'd been silently nibbling the chocolate bars this whole time, now chimed in with chitchat about Chicago's weather and Granny Crumpler's hat and how tall Mae was getting. But Granny wasn't interested. She never took her eyes off Mae.

Mae plastered a nervous smile on her lips. Words seemed to be stuck somewhere on the other side of them.

I wasn't much help either. My mind was racing, but

my face seemed to be frozen in the same ridiculous grin as Mae's. When I shot a sideways glance at Akiko, she looked a lot like Mae. Only there was a bit of chocolate on her bottom lip.

Granny Crumpler never blinked.

"How did you children get here? When do you go back? Who is watching after you? What will—"

"We just got here," I said, giving a quick poke to Mae's ribs. She needed to snap out of it. Granny Crumpler was scary, but we had faced worse. We'd battled against the serpentlike Hisser in Philadelphia. We'd cracked codes. We'd trained with a spy. Why was Mae so nervous about facing off with a stooped, near-sighted little grandmother?

"Yes, we just got here," Mae began slowly, repeating my words like some sort of dopey robot. "Josie, Akiko, and I dropped in for a bit. To see Aunt Willa and Aunt Janet."

"Dropped in?"

"More like swooped in, like fighter planes," said Akiko with a low chuckle.

I stepped on her toe.

"Dropped in," continued Mae. "As in, *Surprise!* We heard there might be some excitement in Chicago. So we decided to come visit."

Granny let out a *Hmph!* and pushed her glasses up the bridge of her nose. She didn't exactly appear convinced.

"So you mean to tell me that you three *children* decided—"

"To visit Janet and me! And we're so glad they did," said Aunt Willa, thankfully reaching out and wrapping Mae's shoulders in a big hug. "This young lady and her friends are going to get some flying lessons. Mae is already such a capable young pilot!"

Mae started to look a little green.

"No! We aren't! I mean . . . Thanks, Aunt Willa, but we won't really have time for too many lessons," babbled Mae. "We have to get back—to Mrs. B and all. Quickly. She worries, you know."

Her voice was high-pitched and nervous. And all her good manners scattered to the wind like planes taking off just beyond us.

"I'm sorry we didn't let you know our plans, Granny," she added. "Next time I'll be sure and write you a letter so you know what's happening."

"I'd appreciate that, Mae Eugenia," she said, pushing her glasses up her nose. "I haven't heard anything from your father lately, and I'm worried."

Three

"WHAT DO YOU MEAN YOU HAVEN'T HEARD from Daddy?" asked Mae, stepping out from Aunt Willa's hug and over to her grandmother's side. "Is he okay?"

Granny Crumpler's voice was low as she kissed Mae's forehead. "It's been a long while since I've received a letter."

Aunt Willa moved closer to Akiko and me. "Mae's father, Howard, is an ambulance driver with the 590th Ambulance Company," she explained. "While he's not an infantryman, he's still risking his life like every other soldier in the war."

In his last letter, Willa said, he'd written about trying to reach a fallen soldier and drag him to safety while German bullets flew at him overhead. "Howard drives right through the battles. And at the same time, he's stopping bleeding and bandaging wounds."

Another time, said Aunt Janet, Howard had written about coming across a White soldier who was lying on the ground and bleeding pretty badly. When he saw Howard, the man called for another medic. He refused to be treated by a Black man, even though Mae's dad could have saved his life. "Mae's daddy said he's fighting two wars: One is the war against Germany and Japan. And the other is the war against segregation at home."

"We call it the Double V campaign," Granny said gently. "Victory overseas and victory right here in America."

Mae's shoulders were shaking, and she buried her face in her grandmother's neck. I wanted to run to her and tell her I understood. My dad's death was the hardest thing I'd ever gone through. And the ache of missing him felt like something was tearing inside my chest. But there was a good chance her dad was safe and alive, just too busy to write a letter home.

"We don't hear a lot from my brother, Tommy, either," said Akiko in a gravelly whisper. "I have no idea whether he is dead or alive. I just have to believe that he's going to come through this war okay. That the good guys win."

Suddenly one of the mechanics working on a plane

behind us started shouting. He rolled out from underneath it and jumped to his feet.

"Listen to that!" he hollered, racing to a radio in the far corner and turning up the volume. "They're saying there's been some kind of explosion in downtown Chicago!"

Akiko and I ran to the radio to hear for ourselves. Aunt Willa and Aunt Janet were right behind us. And Mae and her grandmother followed close on their heels. We gathered in with the other students and mechanics to catch what the announcer was saying.

". . . spies have landed in America! Dropped off by German U-boats along the coast of New York and Florida! They're suspected to be on the loose in downtown Chicago after an explosion this afternoon at the Norden Bombsight factory. . . ."

In the distance, I heard a deep *BOOM* echo across the city.

"Spies?" shouted Aunt Willa. "From the sound of it, they're already making trouble!"

"Let's go, Willa," called Aunt Janet as she raced toward a plane parked on the tarmac. "We can help find them! Before they do more harm!"

Akiko, Mae, and I watched the two pilots tug their goggles over their eyes and adjust their helmets. They were going to fly downtown to investigate.

To fight bad guys.

To help keep innocent people from getting hurt.

To do some good.

"Wait for us!" I hollered, racing toward Aunt Janet's bright red plane.

"There's room for me in there too," croaked Akiko, and we wedged in together in the seat behind Janet. Akiko's Hauntima bag smashed into my hip, so she moved it to her left side. "Let's go!"

Not far from us, Aunt Willa's engine roared to life. I watched Mae as she stood frozen in place, as stiff as one of the flagpoles. She stared after her aunt, and I knew she must have been wrestling with all sorts of worries in her head. Finally, she whipped off the white scarf and waved it in the air to get her aunt's attention. "Me too," she shouted. "I'll go too, Aunt Willa!"

As Mae jumped into the back seat, she returned the scarf to her aunt. Willa quickly wrapped it around her neck. She threw one end over her shoulder with a flourish that reminded me of a Hollywood movie star. Then she passed back a pair of goggles and a helmet for Mae to put on.

I couldn't help but smile as I watched their plane taxi down the runway.

"You'll need this," Aunt Janet shouted to Akiko and me over the engine's noisy growl. And she handed us the same aviator's gear that we saw on Mae. Akiko took the goggles, and I tugged on the leather helmet. "And for goodness' sake, fasten that seat belt tight across the both of you! These are open cockpits. I don't want you two dropping through the clouds like a couple of superheroes who forgot their capes!"

As Aunt Janet turned back to the control panel, Akiko smacked a hand over her mouth to keep from laughing.

"Seat belt fastened!" I shouted. "Let's go!"

Akiko's hair whipped my cheek as we sped down the runway and lined up behind the other planes for our turn to take off. There were biplanes with their sturdy wings stacked on top of each other and small planes that seemed light as hummingbirds. We craned our necks to catch a glimpse of Aunt Willa's sunshine-yellow plane—Aunt Janet said it was called a Piper Cub.

Its wings looked like an oversize Popsicle stick stuck to the plane's roof. Could that thing really fly?

We watched it speed down the runway, then suddenly become airborne. Aunt Willa's white scarf rippled behind her as her plane cleared the trees at the far side of the long airfield, climbing higher and higher. I imagined Mae up there in the seat behind Willa, squeezing her eyes shut and refusing to look down.

"Look at them go!" croaked Akiko. "She's actually doing it!"

"Mae's flying!" I agreed, pounding on Akiko's knee in excitement as we watched her soar up, up, up into the clouds. And with a laugh, I added, "Like a superhero without a cape."

Four

WE ROARED OVER CHICAGO'S STREETS AND parks, rising higher until the scene below us looked like a playroom of toy trucks and cars. The air turned chilly and made my eyes water. Akiko winked at me through her goggles, the wind slicking back her hair like it was wet. I was grateful I had the soft leather helmet. At least my wild curls were mostly under control for once.

Aunt Willa's yellow plane was off to our right and just ahead. The engine droned steadily as we kept an even pace. Flying in planes was totally different from flying as the Infinity Trinity. We were going much faster, for one thing.

And since we were sitting upright, I felt better about looking around and scanning the horizon. When I flew as the Emerald Shield, it was a little like diving into water. My arms got pretty tired after a while. Plus, I always worried about running into a flock of birds and getting a mouth full of feathers. Flying like this, in a plane, seemed to have some advantages.

"Can you see downtown?" hollered Aunt Janet over her shoulder. "It's there."

She pointed up ahead, and I followed the coastline north until I caught sight of tall buildings bumping up alongside Lake Michigan's wide blue water. There it was—downtown Chicago. All at once, over the dull roar of the planes' engines, I heard another unmistakable *BOOM*.

"That's an explosion!" shouted Akiko. "The spies are still at it!"

"Do you think we'll be able to catch them?" I yelled into her ear.

"I sure hope so!" she called back. "Too many people could get hurt if they keep this up!"

Aunt Willa's plane began to roll to the right, the wings tipping gracefully from horizontal to vertical. So Aunt Janet followed suit. As the ground below us suddenly came into clearer view, my stomach started rolling too. I gripped the edge of our cockpit and squeezed my eyes shut.

Once our planes evened out again, I saw we were flying

lower and seemed to be following along the shoreline. As we caught up with Aunt Willa's plane, still off to the right, I noticed that Mae was waving to us.

Akiko and I waved back.

But Mae kept waving. No, she was gesturing. She seemed to be getting more excited with every passing second. Was she trying to tell us something?

"She's pointing up," shouted Akiko. "Why is she doing that? Is it going to rain?"

Akiko and I looked above us. The sky was a cloudless blue. What was Mae trying to say?

"I think she wants us to fly higher," I hollered. "Or maybe they want to?"

"Is she trying to tell us something about the wind?" asked Akiko, yelling into my ear. "I've always said she's a few noodles short of a casserole! A few colors shy of a rainbow! A few clowns less than a circus—"

"No," I called back, emphatically shaking my head. "No talk of clowns. Not after Side-Splitter."

We both winced at the memory of big red noses and bowler hats.

But looking over at Mae gesturing wildly in the neighboring plane, I could not figure out what she was doing. Now she was pointing upward with both hands, her mouth wide open like she was yelling.

I was just turning to Akiko when motion above us

caught my eye. It was followed by the deafening roar of an engine.

"Another plane!" howled Akiko, ducking her head. "Where did that come from?"

"That must have been what Mae was warning us about!" I shouted. "Who is it?"

Aunt Janet was unfazed by our noisy neighbor. She pointed east, toward the water, and called to us over her shoulder.

"See those long ships on Lake Michigan?" she hollered. "Those are aircraft carriers. The navy is using them for practice. They're teaching pilots how to land on moving targets floating on water. They'll get even more practice when they transfer out to the Pacific Ocean."

Akiko and I stared toward the lake. We watched a gray-blue plane dart across the horizon and head toward a flat ship that reminded me a little of a parking lot. The plane sank lower in the sky until it reached the ship; then it made a bouncy landing and rolled to a sudden halt.

"Is that what just flew over our heads?" I shouted up to Aunt Janet. "One of those practice planes?"

She nodded.

"I sure wish they'd let somebody like me fly one of those," Aunt Janet called. "Or Willa—we'd show the Germans a thing or two!"

Up ahead of us, Aunt Willa banked her plane to the

left. It rolled gracefully through the air, its wings making a straight line up and down. And I imagined Mae letting out one of her dramatic gasps as she stared down into the streets below. It looked as if their plane could have slipped between the tall buildings.

Aunt Janet did the same with our plane, and again my stomach tumbled to my throat as we tipped sideways through the sky.

"Hang on, kiddos!" she shouted. Akiko clung to me as the left wing, which was on her side, dipped lower and lower. Leaning as far as I could to the right, I felt like we were about to spill onto the street. Our plane was flying so low and at such an angle, it seemed like Akiko could reach out to a newspaper stand and scoop up a comic book.

"Looks like Willa wants to follow the Chicago River and see what's what!" hollered Aunt Janet over her shoulder. "Keep your eyes open! Tell me if you see anything suspicious!"

Suspicious? I had no idea what to look for. Akiko, Mae, and I already knew spies could come in all shapes and sizes. And they were often what we least expected.

The roar of our engines was louder than ever as we buzzed the bridges over the river. The sound bounced off the brick buildings to our left and right, pounding in my ears as well as my chest. My eyes darted from one structure to the next, eager to spot something of interest.

Ah-choo!

"Allergies again?" I asked Akiko, wondering if there was anything that didn't make her sneeze. She reached into her canvas bag and pulled out a white hankie to blow her nose. But then she started waving her hankie frantically and pointing like Mae had done moments ago.

"Over there, Josie. Look!" she shouted, gesturing to the left, where a plume of gray smoke was rising off a rooftop. "That's definitely suspicious!"

Five

$\mathscr{I}$ SEE IT TOO," I CALLED TO HER. "BUT I DON'T think it's sabotage. I think it's just a guy having a barbecue. Probably hot dogs—Mae says Chicago has a thing for hot dogs."

She leaned farther over the edge as if studying the cook and his grill. Then she nodded in agreement, and we settled back in our seats and continued searching for spies. I caught a glimpse of Mae in the plane across from us. Like Akiko and me, she was scanning for bad guys off both sides of her plane. Surely one of us would catch sight of something that was truly suspicious.

We soared past the last tall building in downtown and into the more open, flat parts of the city. Aunt Willa up ahead of us banked to the left. Our plane followed. The buildings looked different now, lower and much wider. They were like boxes laid on their sides rather than standing upright. Akiko and I kept on the lookout—for training pilots above us and bad guys below.

I was about to shout a question up to Aunt Janet when she suddenly sent our plane into a steep dive. Akiko and I let out matching screams as our stomachs dropped like we were on a roller-coaster ride.

Aunt Willa's plane swooped in beside us now, keeping an even pace as we zoomed over a wide, flat rooftop. The building was the biggest I'd ever seen. It made me wonder what in the world was inside. I leaned forward in my seat, ready to ask Aunt Janet what she thought, when I heard her voice. I quickly realized she must have been speaking to Aunt Willa over the radio.

". . . factory where they make the devices used to drop bombs! I'm sure of it, Willa!" she called. She paused, listening to Aunt Willa's reply. "Right . . . yes, the Norden Bombsight!"

At hearing this, I couldn't help but lean farther over the edge for a better look. Akiko did the same over the left side. The building seemed to go on and on, taking up too many city blocks to even count. What was a bombsight?

And was it important enough to attract spies?

"Right there!" shouted Akiko. And she jabbed a bony elbow into my rib cage, making me jump. As if chasing down spies in an open-cockpit airplane weren't enough to make me jumpy already!

I swung to her side and shoved my head over the edge. "What did you see?"

I couldn't tell exactly where she was looking because of the goggles covering her eyes. But she pointed her finger into the wind at a couple of spots on the pale rooftop below us. I leaned over even farther for a better view.

"Don't fall out, Josie!" she shouted, grabbing my shoulders. "You're not the Emerald Shield right now! You'll drop like a stone!"

I steadied myself, glancing at Aunt Janet to make sure she hadn't caught the mention of my superhero name. There was no way she could have heard us, though, over the whipping wind and Aunt Willa's voice coming through on the radio.

The spots where Akiko was pointing were moving now—two of them. They were yellowish-tan circles, racing along side by side. We were looking down on two straw hats, I realized from this perspective. And beneath the hats were two men dressed in pale summer suits. They had been squatting behind a boxy shed of some sort.

"I see them!" I hollered back to Akiko. "They're running now! But why?"

All at once a door on the rooftop shed burst open, and what seemed to be two security guards came rushing out. Their billy clubs were raised as they looked all around. Finally they caught sight of the two men in the straw hats, who'd taken off at a sprint, and they began to chase after them.

"They've got to be the spies!" yelped Akiko. "Who else would be running around on a bombsight factory's roof right about now!"

We called up to Aunt Janet and pointed out what we were seeing. "Over there! The straw hats," we told her. Aunt Janet nodded and banked our plane to the right. When I glanced across at Mae's plane, I saw her pointing them out to Aunt Willa, too. They rolled right just behind us, then zoomed in low so our two planes were flying side by side. With the sun shining overhead, our T-shaped shadows raced across the factory roof just ahead of us.

"Why did you say *might be spies*, Josie?" hollered Akiko. "Of course they are!"

"We don't know for sure yet," I answered. "We need evidence."

"Evidence?" shouted Akiko. "Like what?"

Suddenly a shot rang out below, followed by three more. The men in suits were hiding behind another boxy shed—it must have been the doorway for the rooftop staircase or something.

"Evidence like that—bullets!" I yelled, clutching Akiko's shoulders tighter. "You're right, Akiko. They must be the spies we heard about on the radio. Should we transform? Although that will be hard to explain to Aunt Janet and Aunt Willa!"

"Not possible!" Akiko said, giving her head a firm shake. "Not with Mae in the other plane! Remember? The three of us have to be together in order to transform into the Infinity Trinity."

Aunt Janet swung our plane off to the right, just as Aunt Willa peeled off to the left. We heard more shots ring out from the rooftop below us, then saw a few more security guards race out of another staircase doorway.

After circling wide, our two planes met up at the far edge of the factory building and again flew in low over the rooftop to catch up with the spies. They were running now, with the four guards chasing after them. As we watched the straw hats separate in opposite directions, we saw the guards scatter too.

"Watch that one!" Akiko called. "He's going off to the right, Aunt Janet!"

I saw the other one head to the left, with two guards trailing behind him. But just as I turned back to Akiko's side, I heard a sound I didn't recognize.

Ping! Ping!

Had we been hit? Our plane's nose shot into the air

and we rocketed skyward. It happened so fast, I felt like I was on the swings at the park. Akiko let out a scream and clutched at our seat belt to hang on. My head was forced back against the headrest, preventing me from lifting it. My body felt heavy, as if all my weight shifted down to my feet.

I strained to catch a glimpse of Mae and Aunt Willa. They seemed to be moving side by side with us again, soaring in an enormous loop through the sky!

"Sometimes pilots pass out doing moves like these," Aunt Janet hollered over her shoulder to us. "Make sure to brace yourselves, and squeeze the muscles in your legs. That'll keep the blood pumping back up to your brains!"

"We're upside down!" I shouted, barely able to push my voice out of my throat. The curls that weren't under my helmet fell like confetti around my face. "Hold on, Akiko!"

But I didn't need to warn her about anything. "Flying in loops might be even better than teleporting," she called back to me. And I didn't have to see her expression to know she was loving the acrobatics. Mae, on the other hand, was probably having a different reaction.

"This is no place for kids," called Aunt Janet. "We've got to get you three back to the hangar and contact the police! Can you believe it—spies in Chicago? What will we see next? Caped superheroes?"

Six

*W*E WERE BACK ON THE GROUND MINUTES later. But that didn't mean we wanted to stay put. Once Mae got her legs working, she followed after her aunts like a determined puppy. But Aunt Willa and Aunt Janet had rushed away from us and into the hangar—to report what we'd seen on the rooftop. One of the mechanics was already dialing the phone as they breathlessly told their stories.

"You've got to let us help," Mae insisted in her usual polite manner. Only louder. They still had their backs to her, but that didn't deter Mae. "Akiko, Josie, and I are smart. We can do things!"

Finally Aunt Willa turned around to face her.

"You can stop shouting, Mae," she said calmly. "We're not up in the clouds anymore. I can hear you just fine. And no, you cannot help us. This is simply too dangerous. Just imagine how I'd explain it to Granny—that I let you all come near these spies. Three children? It's a ridiculous thought!"

Akiko and I tried to help out.

"We're not ordinary kids," Akiko said in her gravelly voice. "We . . . I mean . . . We might surprise you."

"Mae and Akiko are right," I added. "We're just kids, sure. But there's a lot more to us than you realize. We're really good at solving problems! We can operate the radio! We can decode any messages that might come in! And we . . ."

I didn't know how far to go. And by the looks on their faces, neither did Mae and Akiko. Should we admit that we had superpowers? Should we inform them that stopping bad guys was our business? Though that was definitely *not* our motto. Well, maybe it was Akiko's. Mae's motto was probably more along the lines of *Saving innocents—including animals!—is what we do!*

"There's a lot at stake here," insisted Mae, "especially innocent people getting harmed. We can't let that happen, Aunt Willa. So that's why the three of us should . . ."

Her words hung in the air.

We should *what*?

This was a big moment. But none of us was prepared for how to explain it. We hadn't told our families about our superpowers. Mostly this was to protect them from evil-doers like the Hisser and Side-Splitter, who would surely try to harm them to get to us if given the opportunity. But also to keep our families from worrying about us. And from making us sit cooped up indoors all summer.

I tried to signal Mae and Akiko with my eyebrows. Were they okay with our secret identities as the Violet Vortex, the Orange Inferno, and the Emerald Shield being revealed? Had Aunt Willa and Aunt Janet already heard of the Infinity Trinity?

"Somebody needs to fight those spies," began Akiko.

"Right," I agreed, unsure how to say it. "Which is why we should be the ones . . ."

We both turned to Mae. Chicago was her city! These were her aunts!

Surely Mae would be able to think of some way to explain our situation to them. When we were in Philadelphia with my cousin Kay and the Secret Six computer programmers, I was fine doing most of the talking. It was my town, after all. And San Francisco felt like Akiko's show. She knew the neighborhoods, the landmarks, and the names of important buildings. It was great having Akiko drive the bus, so to speak. Or rather, the cable car.

Now it was Mae's turn to lead.

I slid my foot over and poked her shoe, hoping her aunts didn't take notice. Akiko cleared her throat dramatically and urged Mae on with a quick nod of her head.

Mae took a deep breath.

"Aunt Willa and Aunt Janet," she began, "you both know what it's like to have people underestimate you." Shifting her weight from one foot to the other, she pushed on. "Some airports won't allow Black pilots to take off and land. Some people laugh at the idea of women flying planes. So when it comes to Black women pilots? Well, it's beyond what small minds can imagine. Hardly anybody thinks someone who looks like me or you could control one of these Piper Cubs.

"I guess," she went on, "they never heard of Bessie Coleman."

Mae had gotten their attention. Bessie was the first Black woman to take to the skies, and a photograph of her hung on the wall inside the hangar. Aunt Willa and Aunt Janet stood perfectly still. Their eyes never left Mae's face.

"Well, we don't want you underestimating us," Mae said gently. "I mean, I'm not telling you what to do. But it's just . . . Sure, we're kids. But we can do so many things you might not even know about.

"Like Josie, for example. She's so good at math. I bet she could calculate how fast you'd need to fly to make it to Navy Pier in ten minutes—without even using a pencil.

And Akiko, she's so great at ciphers. There isn't a code those spies could use that Akiko couldn't crack."

I felt my cheeks burn.

When I peeked over at Akiko, she was self-consciously tinkering with the clip in her hair.

"And me," continued Mae, "well, I'm still figuring out what I'm good at."

I'd never met anybody so modest. Even though Mae was good at a long list of things, she was much too polite to rattle them off.

"But if you'd just let—"

"She's great at puzzling," interrupted Akiko. And she bumped Mae with her hip. "Not to mention math, eaves-dropping, lock-picking, spy tricks, never sweating, talking to animals, eating pie—"

"Mae is amazing," I said, taking my turn to interrupt. "There's nobody like her."

Aunt Willa stuffed her silky white scarf into her pocket and sighed.

"I do agree with these girls, Janet," she said. "Mae has been an exceptional flying student. She's gone up with me many times, executing wonderful takeoffs and landings. And using that Link Trainer over there, she's shown me how she can bank left and right, roll out of a chase, and soar straight up to eternity. And as of this afternoon over downtown Chicago, she has experience spiraling down like a corkscrew and even looping like a curlicue in cursive writing.

"She's smart, safety conscious, and serious about piloting. I would call Mae one of my best students," said Aunt Willa with a smile, "despite the fact that she's just a—"

"CHILD!"

Seven

LIKE AN ANGRY SEAGULL, THAT CALL pierced the air.

"Granny Crumpler!" whispered Mae. "She's still here!"

Aunt Willa and Aunt Janet snapped to attention. In stunned silence, the five of us turned and watched Granny's stooped shape slam the door of a shiny Ford sedan. Even the mechanics and students inside the hangar stopped moving for fear of drawing Granny's sharp eye.

And as before, her tiny form cast a long shadow across the tarmac toward us.

"Mae Eugenia Crumpler," she announced, "I cannot

tell these grown women what to do. But as for you, my job is to keep you safe. And with all the whatnot happening across this city, that means you need to be close by my side. Your little friends, too. All three of you escapees from that summer camp."

Mae, Akiko, and I began to protest. But our complaints were quickly lost as the mechanics and students began rushing out to talk to Aunt Willa and Aunt Janet. Shouts and exclamations of surprise filled the air like planes in flight.

"You kids should go with Granny Crumpler," Aunt Willa said, ushering Mae toward the waiting car. Akiko and I followed, trying to hear their conversation.

"And, Mae, please know that I don't underestimate your abilities," she declared, stepping one of her tall boots onto the running board that stretched the length of the car's side. "You're quite possibly the fastest learner I've ever taught. Once you overcome those worries—your fear of heights or whatever it is—I know you'll be a great flier."

Granny climbed behind the wheel and revved the car engine. And just like that, Mae, Akiko, and I slipped into the back seat and met our fate. No more soaring in planes with daring aunts. No more chasing fearlessly after German spies. No more racing breathlessly over Chicago buildings.

"I've got stacks of books in the apartment," Granny began, her head barely clearing the steering wheel. Her eyes were piercing as she watched us in the rearview mirror.

I could imagine what it felt like to be in her library. Just one look from Granny Crumpler could probably shush an entire building. "I'll need you three to sort the fiction from the nonfiction."

Akiko rolled her eyes. "Hauntima's ghost!" she complained in her low rumble—a whisper that wasn't quite a whisper. I was grateful the car's windows were down and the rushing air was muffling Akiko's voice. "Instead of catching bad guys and protecting innocent people, we're going to be stuck piling up dusty old books!"

Granny wasn't done.

"And after the books, I'll need you three to help fix supper. One to roll out the biscuits, another to slice the tomatoes, a third to open the canned fish."

I pinched my nose at the thought of smelly fish from a can. "I call dibs on tomatoes," I whispered.

Mae followed with a quick, "Biscuits!"

"No way!" croaked Akiko, her whisper louder than ever. "I am not getting stuck with smelly sardines!"

Granny Crumpler *still* wasn't done.

"And after that, you girls will tend to my neighbor's Victory Garden. The heat is bothering him, so I told him you girls are young and capable. He's got chickens, too. Their droppings are the perfect thing to work into the soil. Chicken waste is pure gold."

"Hauntima's g—"

Mae and I clamped our hands over Akiko's mouth. The last thing we needed was to put ourselves on Granny Crumpler's bad side.

"We'll be happy to help," piped up Mae in her courteous way. "You just rest when we get home. Josie, Akiko, and I will take care of everything."

Akiko couldn't speak, but her eye rolling said plenty.

And I had to agree with her.

"Spies, Mae. *Spies!*" I whispered as we slipped our hands away from Akiko's mouth, confident that she wouldn't erupt again like a dangerous volcano. "Threatening Chicago! And instead of catching them, we're going to be stuck inside your grandmother's apartment!"

Mae gave a frantic shrug.

"Granny gets what Granny wants," she whispered. "She might look delicate and frail, but that woman is as tough as Aunt Willa's leather boots. And she has something close to superpowers with her hearing. She wakes at the sound of a mosquito! So there's no way we can sneak back over to the airport and my aunts tonight. Granny would catch us!"

I stared out at the buildings rushing by. The air from the open windows whipped my hair in all directions, almost as if we were flying. I itched for the opportunity to transform again. Whether wearing my emerald cape and gliding over Chicago as part of the Infinity Trinity, or donning that aviator's helmet and soaring in Aunt Janet's plane, I couldn't wait to be airborne. There was no feeling like it.

"I just want to fly," I said softly. "Like my dad."

He loved being up in the clouds. That's why he signed up to serve in the war. He knew he could help out that way—flying planes, protecting ships and bases, chasing down bad guys. I missed him so much.

Mae and Akiko went quiet too. I figured they were probably thinking about their families, just like I was. The people we loved were never far from our minds. And Mae and Akiko both had so much to worry about.

Mae was eager to get word from her daddy, to know that he was safe driving ambulances into battles over in France. And Akiko already knew that her brother being in the 442nd Regimental Combat Team meant he was sent into the most dangerous fighting. Worry must have gnawed at their stomachs all the time.

"We'll figure something out," I whispered. "We've beaten bigger opponents, right? The Infinity Trinity is not about to let a little grandmother keep us from protecting innocents, fighting for justice, and doing some good."

Ah-choo!

Akiko blew her nose, then stuffed her hankie back into her bag.

"That's right, Josie. The Infinity Trinity," she said, clearly allergic to something blowing through the open windows, "is not going to let a granny keep us stuck inside an apartment either."

Mae gave us a nervous smile.

"We won't be stuck inside the whole time," she said, sounding apologetic. "We'll be *outside*, too. With the chicken poop."

Eight

$\mathscr{I}$T WAS NEARLY MIDNIGHT BY THE TIME WE'D
finished all the chores Granny Crumpler had set out for
us. I was the last to soak in the bathtub, taking my time to
scrape the dirt out from under my fingernails.

Working in their neighbor's Victory Garden—a plot of
land about the size of the whole apartment that was produc-
ing tomatoes, peppers, cucumbers, and all kinds of other
vegetables to feed the community—hadn't been so bad. I
liked being busy.

While we were tying back zucchini plants and pluck-
ing weeds, I'd let my mind play through all the different

thoughts bumping around in there. The radio reports had said downtown was quiet, but I wondered what those spies had in store for tomorrow.

"Which comic book do you want to read?" Akiko asked as I walked back into Mae's bedroom from the tub. She was stretched on the floor and pulling out a surprising number of things from her bag. "I've got Hopscotch, Hauntima, Nova the Sunchaser. And, of course, a few Zenobia issues."

"We've got to get that moonstone ring to her," I said, running a towel through my wet hair. "The moonstones gave Mrs. B and Astra strength. Maybe having that ring back on her finger will restore Zenobia's energy."

"We can only hope," Akiko said, pulling a small wooden box from her bag and lifting the lid. Inside was the ring. Even in the dim light of Mae's room, the milky-white gem glimmered. "Zenobia and the others can't wait much longer."

"No more delays," agreed Mae, her arms full of pillows. "Once we figure out what's happening here in Chicago, we'll get ourselves to Paris to find them. The league of secret heroes is counting on us!"

Mae lined up three pillows and three blankets next to each other on the lavender rug. As polite as Mae was, she wouldn't dare take the bed for herself. Or choose between Akiko and me to take it. So from the looks of it, she'd decided that all three of us would sleep on the floor.

"Let's read these comic books together," I said, plopping

down and looking more closely at the issue featuring Hauntima battling a scorpion. "Our favorite superheroes use all kinds of tricks to defeat bad guys. Maybe we can pick up some ideas."

Mae nodded, studying the cover of her comic book. It featured Nova the Sunchaser using her powers of super-intelligence to defeat the Invisible Itch.

"Rescuing Zenobia and the other superheroes is top priority," Mae said. "But should we let Room Twelve know about the spies in Chicago? If things get dangerous here, we might need Mrs. B to put some agents on it while we're off saving the world!"

Akiko flipped through the pages of her Hopscotch comic book. She was munching on Lorna Doone cookies as she read, and I could hear her raspy breathing with every bite. I couldn't help but smile as I reached for the package too. There was something comforting in Akiko's noisy habits and Mae's polite hospitality. And in the fact that Granny Crumpler's favorite cookies were the exact same as mine.

"We've got to come up with a way to let Room Twelve know," Akiko said, dusting crumbs from her page. "We've never been the ones to send them a message. They've been the ones to find us."

Mae stopped her cookie halfway to her mouth.

"Hold on," she began. "I need to make a couple of things

clear about contacting Room Twelve. We are *not* transforming into the Infinity Trinity in the room next to my grandmother. And we are *not* sneaking out of this apartment," she said, her voice low but firm. "We can't teleport anywhere, can't invite Mrs. B and Astra to visit us here, can't have Hopscotch zooming around here on her scooter, can't ask Hauntima to fly around. No way. Nope. *Uh-uh.* Not with Granny Crumpler on the other side of that wall."

Clearly Mae was worried about getting caught. And to be honest, I was too.

"Well, do you have any ideas?" croaked Akiko. "Anything that won't get us in trouble with your granny?"

"She's right, Mae." I shrugged. "You've got a long list of what we can't do. What *can* we do? Make a phone call? Write a letter?"

Mae stared at her comic book, concentrating on the illustrations. I couldn't tell if she was ignoring us or trying to form a plan. After a moment or two, she tapped the colorful cover and sat up straighter.

"Look at this!" she whispered, holding up the page. All I could see was an image of Nova the Sunchaser's plane, angular and sleek. "Does it remind you of something?"

Akiko tilted her head to one side.

"That long triangle looks like a slice of pie," Akiko said. "And it's making me hungry. I didn't take a single bite of that canned fish. No offense to your granny, Mae—"

"Not only pie," I interrupted. "It also looks like a paper airplane."

Mae's eyes lit up.

"What if we wrote Nova a note?" she wondered, her voice barely above a whisper. "And folded it up like her plane? We could sail it out the window."

"You think Nova would somehow find it? And know who we are?" I asked.

I was skeptical, but Akiko seemed to be warming up to the idea.

"It's possible, Josie. Hauntima knew that we needed her—even before we did," she said. "And she appeared out of thin air to help us. Hopscotch was the same: We spoke her name, and there she was."

"But that was only when we were the Infinity Trinity," I said. "I don't know if this stuff works when we're just plain old Akiko, Mae, and Josie."

Mae jumped to her feet and raced over to a shelf in the corner. When she returned, she was holding a stack of blank sheets of paper. She plopped back down on her pillow and began folding and creasing the paper into long triangular shapes, like airplanes. Akiko joined in.

"What about the message?" she asked, turning to Mae. "What if some stranger walking down the street finds our note?"

"We have to write it in secret code," Mae said. "We

don't want anyone taking our note to Granny."

We whispered ideas back and forth, trying to decide exactly what to say and how to say it. Should we tell Nova about the spies? Or should we ask her to help us get back to Room Twelve? Should we scramble the letters or write in open code, the way the Doll Lady did in San Francisco? Or set up a five-by-five grid like the one in the note about Side-Splitter and his clowns?

Now it was my turn to jump up. When I returned to the room, carrying a small cup of milk and a cotton napkin from the kitchen, Akiko and Mae looked baffled.

"Josie, this is no time for dipping cookies," Akiko whisper-shouted. "We've got to communicate with Nova."

I ignored her and sank the triangular tip of the napkin into my glass. Then I pulled it out and began writing on a sheet of paper in front of me:

CALLING NOVA THE SUNCHASER!
SPIES THREATENING CHICAGO!
∞ Δ

The white milk soaked into the white paper, but not before we could just make out the lettering. I heard Akiko whispering the words as I moved across the page. Once it dried, the page looked untouched—a blank sheet.

Now it was her turn to have doubts. "Invisible ink?

But how will Nova know what to do?" Akiko looked first into my face and then into Mae's. "We're experts at secret messages. But not everyone knows to hold the paper near a flame in order to read it."

Mae's face broke into a wide smile, and she looked the happiest I'd seen her since we arrived in Chicago. Flinging an arm around Akiko's shoulders, she pressed tighter into our triangle.

"We don't have to worry about her figuring out what to do," Mae whispered in a voice almost as loud as Akiko's. "Because Nova the Sunchaser has superintelligence. She built her own airplane, after all. When she gets this message, she'll know exactly how to read it!"

Nine

THE LAST THING WE DID BEFORE TURNING out the lights was to fold the invisible-ink message into the shape of Nova the Sunchaser's paper airplane. The long angles came to a sharp point in the front of the plane, and raised flaps on the back gave it lift. Akiko folded it, I went over every edge to make the creases sharp, and Mae shot it out her bedroom window into the night sky.

But when we woke in the morning, Nova wasn't there shaking our shoulders and rousting us out of bed. Instead, it was the shrill whistle of Granny Crumpler's teakettle that jarred us awake.

"You children did an excellent job on the chores yesterday," Granny called from the stove. "I want you getting started on a few more for me today. Now wash your faces and tidy that room. Then you need to get out the door."

Akiko and I followed Mae into the kitchen, where her grandmother was piling waffles and eggs onto plates. Granny's hair was perfect, and her dress looked neatly pressed. It seemed like she'd been up for hours already. When did this woman sleep?

"What kind of chores, Granny?" asked Mae. While Akiko and I could barely keep from falling back asleep, Mae was already the picture of sunshine. Looking from Granny to her, I realized where she got her always-put-together ways.

I pushed my messy hair out of my eyes and passed the syrup to Akiko, whose own hair was pointing in all directions. I tried not to laugh.

"I need you children to deliver those books you sorted. Drop them over at the public library on Professor Intrepid Street," she said. "You can take the bicycles from out back. They have baskets big enough to hold a whole stack. The librarians will be happy to see you."

Mae beamed at Akiko and me. This latest errand, she whispered, was our ticket to freedom from Granny's watchful eye. The three of us wolfed down our waffles, raced through our morning chores, then bolted out the door.

"Look for signs of Nova the Sunchaser," Akiko huffed as we pedaled away from Granny's apartment building. "She might have gotten our note by now. She could be looking for us."

My legs were pumping as we ferried the heavy books across town. But I wasn't nearly as breathless as Akiko. I could hear her raspy breathing behind me. Even Mae, up ahead of us in the lead, kept turning around to check on our pink-cheeked friend.

"Should I slow down, Akiko?" Mae called over her shoulder. "I don't want you getting overheated. These books are so heavy—"

"I'm fine," she hollered up to us. "But I think"—*puff, puff*—"I'm starting"—*puff, puff*—"to appreciate short stories."

Once we'd stacked the thick books on the wooden desk inside the library, Mae dashed back down the steps to our bikes. Akiko and I were still catching our breath as we tried to keep up.

"There's no time to waste," Mae said quietly, her fingers already wrapped around the grips on the handlebars. "We've got to ride out to the airport. Maybe today my aunts will let us help chase down those spies."

"And we've got to think of other ways to reach Room Twelve and tell them what's going on," I said, looking up into the morning sky and searching for Nova the Sunchaser's white glider plane. "If Nova hasn't gotten our secret message, then we'll have to figure out the next step ourselves."

Akiko said she knew we could. We'd done so much already, she pointed out. But I couldn't stop the hiccup of worry in the pit of my stomach. When we were fighting the Hisser and first learning to use our powers, Hauntima was there to guide us. When Side-Splitter and his army of clowns nearly overwhelmed us, Hopscotch appeared and showed us her secrets to defeat him.

What would happen now, here in Chicago, if there were no superheroes to help us catch these bad guys?

We pushed off from the library and began riding again, each of us lost in thought as we pedaled for the airport. I loved feeling the rush of wind through my hair. After flying in a plane and zooming downhill in a cable car, bicycling was probably my favorite way to get around—that is, when I wasn't wearing a cape, mask, and boots.

A half hour or so later, we saw a sign for the airport. Mae led us past the low steel buildings and wooden sheds to her aunts' hangar. Planes roared above us, and Akiko and I couldn't stop the urge to duck every time another one passed. They sounded close enough to touch.

"We're early," she observed as we parked our bikes. The classroom desks and tool-covered tables stood empty, waiting for the students and teachers to return. We could see pilots and mechanics across the way, but no sign of Mae's aunts.

Akiko and I peeked into the flightless airplane they called the Link Trainer. This was where Mae had been sitting yesterday, with Aunt Willa. The dashboard was covered in dials and gauges, just like the cockpit of a real plane. Akiko reached in and touched the controls.

"Show us what you know, Mae," I said, opening the Trainer's door and waving her toward the seat. "How do you fly one of these things? I can't imagine getting the hang of this."

Mae climbed in, saying it was nothing, that anybody could learn. But we knew it wasn't so easy. "If any knucklehead could do this, the sky would be full of planes," Akiko said, picking up a toy model of a Piper Cub that was sitting on a desk nearby. Mae told us she'd been taking flying lessons for years.

"Here's how we take off," she said, her voice bubbling with excitement. "Once you've checked the propeller up front, checked the wings right and left"—and here she turned her head, first to one side, then the other—"then you check your controls." She paused, touching the circular dials on the panel in front of her.

"You fix your eyes on a spot down the runway," she continued, looking through the windshield and pointing across the room toward an open window. Her gaze went all the way outside and onto the tarmac. Akiko and I pressed in so our heads were touching Mae's on either side. We were imagining it with her. "We roll down the runway. We pick up more speed, faster and faster. Then we use the stick to pull the nose up, up, up and lift—"

"Hauntima's ghost!" shouted Akiko, fumbling the toy plane.

"It's not that scary," Mae said. "Your stomach kind of drops, but it's not—"

"I'm not scared of flying," Akiko hollered again. "I'm scared of that! Look!"

We followed where her finger was pointing, out the window and beyond, to the parked planes. And that's when we saw it.

One round straw hat.

Followed by another.

They topped two figures in pale suits like the ones we'd seen yesterday on the rooftop. And they were slinking beneath the wings of the flight school's planes.

"The spies," I whispered. "They've come looking for your aunts."

"They must not have liked Aunt Willa and Aunt Janet getting so close to them yesterday," Mae said in a tight voice. "So they decided to track them down!"

The hats weaved from one aircraft to the next, passing more Piper Cubs, the PT-19s, and the shiny silver AT-6 Texan. When they reached Aunt Willa's plane, one of the men touched the bullet hole on the underside of her left wing. The other man stepped over for a closer inspection, then nodded to his partner.

"And unfortunately," said Akiko in her not-so-quiet whisper, "they've found them!"

Ten

$\mathcal{B}$EFORE WE COULD EVEN MOVE, SHOUTS erupted from the runway like engines backfiring. We saw the men in the straw hats take off running, then heard the distinct call of a woman's voice.

"That's Aunt Willa," gasped Mae. "She's in danger!"

Mae scrambled out of the flight trainer, and together the three of us rushed to the window for a better look. We could barely hear each other now as one of the planes—a big blue one—roared to life nearby.

"I thought we were the only ones here," I called over the noise. "Whose plane is that? It's starting to taxi down the runway!"

We watched as the blue plane sped away. I glimpsed something painted on its front but couldn't tell what it was.

"Come on," Mae said, ducking low and slipping out of the hangar. "We've got to make sure my aunt is okay."

Akiko and I tiptoed along close behind, the three of us holding on to one another's arms and shoulders as we moved together underneath the wide wings of the parked airplanes. The tarmac was still again, and we seemed to be the only people around.

"Where did she go?" I asked, searching in all directions.

"And those men in the straw hats. I know they're the bad guys from yesterday," croaked Akiko. "Where are they?"

The three of us looked all around the airfield for any signs of familiar faces—good or bad. The only sound was the noisy buzz of the blue plane as it cleared the barn at the far end of the runway and soared away from us.

A moment later, it was gone.

Suddenly Mae gasped.

She was pointing at a piece of silky white fabric that was billowing in the wind. It slipped along the runway like a shimmering ribbon come to life. And not far from it was a pair of aviator's goggles.

"Her scarf," Mae whispered, unable to move her feet and chase after it. "That's Aunt Willa's scarf. And those must be Aunt Janet's goggles—she loaned them to Akiko yesterday."

"They've got your aunts," I said, my voice so shaky that

I could barely speak. "Those bad guys. They've kidnapped Willa and Janet!"

Akiko scrambled over the tarmac and scooped up the goggles and the white scarf. She raced back to us, holding them out for Mae to examine.

Mae squeezed her eyes shut. There was no doubt.

"What's going to happen to your aunts?" I asked. "Where are they taking them?"

Panting to catch her breath, Akiko shoved the items into her Hauntima bag. Then she silently stuck her hand out. Mae and I did the same, stacking our hands on top of one another's and forming our familiar tight triangle.

"Answers will come later," Akiko said. "But for right now, we've got to go!"

"We've got to stop these bad guys," I agreed with a nod.

And in a voice I could barely catch, Mae whispered, "Innocents are in danger."

Streams of purple, green, and orange wrapped around us, and the familiar golden light shot skyward. When the swirling hurricane fell away, we dropped back to the ground transformed into the Infinity Trinity. Then, diving into the air, we took off eastward into the morning sky like a squad of fighter pilots.

"We've never chased after a plane before!" Akiko shouted as our capes snapped in the wind. "Do you think we can catch that thing?"

As we flew in formation—Mae at the lead and Akiko and I flanking her on either side—I squinted my eyes and studied the blue speck in the air far ahead of us. I tried to do the math in my head.

"That plane is bigger than the ones we were in yesterday," I hollered. "I bet it goes twice as fast."

We picked up speed, leaning into the wind and pushing with all our might. I could see Lake Michigan come into view now off to our right. And the tall buildings of downtown were rising up ahead of us. How would we ever catch up with the spies in their blue plane? And what would happen to Aunt Willa and Aunt Janet if we didn't?

Like yesterday, we followed the shoreline north until we reached the edge of downtown, where the buildings stood taller than structures in the outlying regions. I was trying to think through a plan for chasing down that plane when suddenly my thoughts were interrupted by something shrieking through the sky above us.

"What was that?" I yelled.

It wasn't a plane but more like an enormous bird of prey. And it was so loud and so close, I could feel the vibrations in my bones.

"I don't know!" answered Mae. "But we can't turn back."

"Right," shouted Akiko, pointing up ahead as the blue plane banked to the east, toward the lake. "We can't lose those spies! Mae's aunts are in there!"

"You mean the Violet Vortex," I called, correcting Akiko. "Remember not to use our real names! It puts too many people in danger!"

Akiko started to apologize, but before she got too far, another plane flashed in the sunlight above us. Only this one was almost silent, slicing through the air like a white dart.

"We're not alone up here," hollered Mae. "Let's be ready for anything."

My heart pounded so hard, I could hear it knocking in my ears. And my eyes jumped nervously as I scanned the skies all around us, looking out for the blue plane up ahead and whatever else might dive at us from the left or right.

Suddenly the silent white plane darted across our path again. It was all sharp angles and long lines. But its shape seemed ghostly, as if it might disappear in the sun's glare. The pointed edges reminded me of a paper airplane, like the one we'd folded last night when we launched our secret message out the window. I watched as it looped upward and over us, coiling around our path like a spring.

"Infinity Trinity!" came a voice from the plane. "Be careful!"

Eleven

$\mathcal{T}$HE GLIDER SWOOPED IN ON MY LEFT SIDE now and kept pace beside us. Sleek and silent, it was completely white except for a symbol painted just beneath the cockpit window: a blazing orange sun with yellow beams radiating out from the center.

"That's her!" gasped Mae. "Nova the Sunchaser!"

"She got our message!" yelled Akiko, punching a fist in the air.

"Nova?" I called to her, hardly believing my eyes. "Is it really you?"

Suddenly two military planes zoomed past us. The force of

their wake blew me backward, and I nearly bumped into Mae.

"We've got to talk!" Nova hollered. "This is too dangerous—"

"Those spies we told you about in the note," Mae shouted to Nova. "We're chasing them. We think they've got my aunts on board their plane!"

Nova nodded that she understood. But behind the round circles of her mask, she kept her eyes looking forward, watching for any more close calls with those planes. And, I assumed, watching out for tall buildings, too.

Even though her long ponytail whipped in the air behind her, Nova's form was as ghostly as her plane. It reminded me of Hopscotch and Hauntima. Whatever had drained their powers was sapping away strength from Nova the Sunchaser too.

"They're in that blue plane," Akiko called, pointing into the distance far ahead of us. "We can't let it get away!"

But before we could lead Nova there, a burst of light suddenly flashed in the sky over the lake. And with it came a thudding *KA-BOOM!* that made me want to cover my ears.

"Tell Room Twelve!" I yelled to Nova. "There's something bad brewing here in Chicago. The league of secret heroes should know!"

Another explosion boomed to the west, rattling the buildings all around us.

"They do know," answered Nova. "And that's why I've come to warn you!"

"Warn us?" hollered Mae. "Warn us about what?"

Nova shot into the sky and looped again. This time she settled on the other side of us, flying steady off Akiko's right side. Honking horns and a noisy commotion rose off the streets below us as I strained to hear Nova's words.

"But it's too late," she called to us. "He's here."

My mouth went dry as another explosion, this one louder than the others, boomed behind us. My eardrums thudded inside my head, not only from the noise but from the force, too.

"*He?*" I managed to shout, thoughts of Side-Splitter and the Hisser racing through my mind. "Who is *he*?"

Before Nova could answer, a frightening screech pierced the air. The sound stung not only my ears but my whole body. And a moment later, an enormous metallic shape crossed over our heads.

"Watch out!" warned Mae. "It's some kind of bird!"

We made a sharp turn to the left, dropping lower and skirting the sides of a tall office building as we flew over the Chicago River.

"It flies like a bird," called Akiko, sneaking glances over her shoulder. "But it's shiny like an airplane. What could it be?"

I was finding it hard to know where to focus my attention. It was challenging enough to manage flying in open areas. But doing it in a busy downtown with lots of tall buildings popping up on all sides was nerve-racking. And while the menacing shape above us rattled me, I didn't want to lose sight of the spies hovering on the horizon. Mae's aunts were in real danger!

"After that plane," Mae called. "We can't let them out of our sight!"

Screech!

The metal bird suddenly raced ahead of us, darting across our path and toward the open lake off to our right. A sense of danger washed over me. This bird was surely another supervillain, like Side-Splitter and the Hisser.

As I turned, I could see Navy Pier and the training ships on the water now. The sky was full of pilots learning to land and take off, in preparation for battles over in Europe and the Pacific. Were they ready to battle an enemy right here? Over Lake Michigan?

"Whatever that thing is," I called, "it's going after those training pilots! We've got to help keep them safe!"

We dove faster through the air and began chasing after the menacing metallic bird. We banked east now, shooting away from the tall buildings and into the open air over the lake. Small planes hummed above us, and I worried about all the pilots who were still learning how to fly. Were they nervous, like Mae had been?

"This bird is probably working with the spies," shouted Mae, "to disrupt the war effort here in Chicago. Just like the radio reports said!"

"What about those ships on the water?" called Akiko.

"Do you think it's trying to keep our pilots from training?"

"There's so much they could attack," Mae said. "The training pilots. The Norden Bombsight factory. All the places where they make torpedoes and parachutes and airplane engines—the list is endless!"

"We've got to stop it," I called as the sinister metal shape swooped after the training pilots. Its movements reminded me of a dangerous gargoyle come to life.

With Nova keeping pace, we raced lower over the water, hoping to draw the villain's attention toward us and away from the vulnerable pilots and the long ships.

Suddenly the metal bird looped through the sky and seemed to redirect itself. Its wingspan looked enormous as it flapped over the lake, closer and closer. All at once, I realized it was flying right for us! From its sharp beak came another shrill screech, reminding me of an eagle about to seize its prey.

And *we* were it.

"That's the Metallic Falcon!" shouted Nova, and she turned us away from Lake Michigan and back into the forest of tall buildings. I'd never flown so fast. We wove a path left and right, like we were racing through an obstacle course. "And I don't think he's out to get those training pilots!

"I'd say he's out to get you!"

Thirteen

THE METALLIC FALCON WAS NOWHERE IN sight. But Akiko and I still turned around and around, searching the skies for any sign of him. Mae stood frozen, focused on some spot on the horizon. Her face looked stricken.

"What is it?" I said, tugging on her arm. "Tell us!"

Mae rubbed at her temples with her purple-gloved hands and squeezed her eyes shut. It looked as if she had a migraine headache. But I imagined reading that terrible villain's mind was even worse.

"I see what he's seeing," she began, her breathing fast.

"The Metallic Falcon! He's laughing. No! No, no, no! He has my aunts. And he says he'll use them to destroy"—she paused, as if trying to catch her breath—"to destroy the Infinity Trinity!"

Mae dropped her hands from her head and put them on her knees. She bent over, panting as if she'd just finished running a race. The vision seemed to be gone now, and her voice sounded exhausted.

"They're in real danger," said Nova, putting her arm around Mae's shoulder. "Now they're part of the Metallic Falcon's sinister game of chess."

She turned to the three of us, pulling Akiko and me in close too.

"Do not lose heart," she began, her appearance ghostly. I knew her powers were being sapped, just like Hauntima's and Hopscotch's, and I had to fight the urge to take her hand and hold on tight. "This supervillain is targeting you for a reason: because you're smart, you're strong, and you're capable. Bullies always go after the ones they see as a threat."

Akiko made a noise that wasn't exactly a cough.

Mae gasped.

I tried to stand up straighter, wanting to believe Nova's words.

"If this weren't the case," she went on, "then he wouldn't even bother. But as you saw today, he wants the battle. He wants to finish off the Infinity Trinity."

"But why us?" croaked Akiko. "Because we're the last superheroes?"

A groan nearby caught Nova's attention. She looked over at a plane beside us, then back to our trio. Her voice was clear despite her fading form.

"Because you're our best hope," she said. "So many of us are nearly powerless. You've seen Mrs. B and Astra, how they were without their moonstones. Drained. The forces of evil have sapped us, left us shells of the superheroes we once were. And that's just the few of us who remain. So many others have been taken.

"You three," she said, giving each of our hands a squeeze, "working on your own as individual fighters, but even more, working together as one—you must save us."

Another moan went up nearby, only louder this time. And now all of us turned to see where it was coming from. I raced over—to one of the downed planes. Mae and Akiko were right beside me.

"The pilot sounds injured," Akiko said. "Can you tell how badly he's hurt?"

We looked into the cockpit. The pilot wore the same brown leather helmet as Aunt Willa, and the goggles were just like the ones Aunt Janet had used. The image of Akiko holding up the goggles and the white scarf she'd found on the runway burned in my mind like a hot flame. That was the moment when we realized Mae's aunts had been kidnapped.

"We should make sure he's breathing okay," I said, lifting off the pilot's goggles. His head lolled to the side.

"He's been knocked out," whispered Mae. "And look—there's a little blood over his eye."

"He must have hit his head," Akiko said, her voice gravelly and low. "But it doesn't look too bad."

Nova appeared on the other side of the cockpit. She leaned in to study the pilot's wound. Then she reached one of her yellow-gloved hands forward and touched the shoulder of the pilot's leather jacket.

"This is no ordinary pilot," Nova whispered, her eyes darting from my face to Akiko's, then Mae's. Even though she was weakened and fading, Nova's expression seemed sparked with new energy.

"What do you mean, Nova?" I asked. "Who is he?"

"Not *he*," she said, nodding toward the pilot's sleeping face. "*She!* This pilot is a woman. She's a WASP!"

Mae's hand shot to her mouth, and Akiko let out a few sneezes.

Ah-choo! Ah-choo! Ah-choo!

"A who?" I asked, gently slipping the pilot's leather helmet from her head. "Do you mean the Winter Wasp? That superhero whose sting turns bad guys to ice?"

Nova shook her head and pointed toward a cloth patch

that was sewn on the pilot's brown jacket, over her heart. It featured a small pixie with curly yellow horns and long blue wings, along with aviator's goggles and a leather helmet. And the pixie's boots were tall and fiery, just like Nova's. Just like Aunt Willa's, too.

"The patch is the symbol for the WASPs," Nova said in an excited, bewildered tone. "This aviator belongs to the Women Airforce Service Pilots—WASPs. They fly all kinds of planes across the country—"

"Women aren't allowed to fly for the war," interrupted Akiko. "Mae's aunt Willa and aunt Janet couldn't sign up to fly against the Nazis. Everybody knows flying is just for men."

Nova shook her head.

"The WASPs are different," she said. "They can't battle Nazis in a dogfight or drop bombs over Germany, but they do risk their lives flying planes for the war. Judging by how new this aircraft looks, this WASP must have been delivering it from a factory to an air base."

Tiny stitching in black thread curved around the base of the pilot's patch. I could tell it spelled something, but I wasn't near enough to read it. Mae leaned in closer and squinted.

"It says 'Avenger Field,' I think," she said, looking up at Nova. "What's that?"

"It sounds like a superhero playground," said Akiko.

Nova stepped away and headed back toward her glider. Her shape was like a phantom's, flickering in the afternoon sunshine.

"Avenger Field is where the WASPs train to fly," she told us. Then she climbed into the cockpit of her plane. "I ask that the three of you, please, see her home safely. The last thing we need is another pilot kidnapped by that bird-brained villain. I must rest for a bit—my strength is nearly gone. But know that I'm tracking you. And I'll make sure Room Twelve never loses touch with the Infinity Trinity."

Fourteen

$\mathcal{N}$OVA TOOK OFF JUST AS THE WASP PILOT began to come around. I had no idea what we were going to say to her, so I bumped Mae with my hip and whispered that she was doing the talking. Akiko agreed, and we both scooted backward just a few inches.

Mae let out a little *ahem.*

The pilot looked all around her, confused.

"What?" she whispered, more to herself than to us. "Where am I?"

She sat up with a start and began checking her dashboard's dials and gadgets.

"The plane!" she said to herself, looking off toward the opposite wing. "What happened to my plane?"

As she turned to the side where we were standing, she caught her breath. We must have been quite a sight, with our capes shimmering in vivid orange, purple, and green. And our masks weren't exactly like the goggles she and the other pilots wore. I peeked down into the cockpit at her boots. I wondered what she'd think of our colorful ones.

"Your plane went down," Mae told her in a quiet, calm voice. "But you're okay, and that's what matters most."

"My plane went down?" the pilot said with a nervous glance toward the engine. "I've got to get back up. It's my job to fly my plane where it needs to be—all in one piece, you know?"

Mae, Akiko, and I looked at each other. The Metallic Falcon had done a number on the propeller, and patches on both wings were blackened from his heat beams. The glass in the windshield was shattered like a spiderweb. Who knew if the engine was damaged? My guess was that it had taken a direct hit from that evil bird.

"If it's wrecked," she said, quickly getting worked up, "then I'm wrecked too!"

"We're here to help you," I said, matching my voice to Mae's calm and steady tone. "Please don't worry. We'll get you home safe and sound. And we'll make sure your plane's all fixed up too."

The pilot put her hands to each side of the cockpit, as if trying to steady herself.

"Whoa, why's everything spinning?" she asked, and I noticed her coloring was off.

"Hauntima's ghost! She's not looking so hot," Akiko whispered. Then, leaning toward the pilot, she said, "Hey, wait! Don't pass out on us. What's your name?"

The pilot rattled her head back and forth, as if trying to wake up. The cut over her right eyebrow must have hurt.

"I'm Baessler. Mildred Jane Baessler," she said, sounding a little groggy. "But everyone calls me Jane."

"Stay with us, Jane," said Mae, her voice pleading. "We're going to take care of you! So don't pass out!"

But pass out she did. Her head fell back on the seat, and she went silent.

"What are we going to do?" croaked Akiko. "Nova said we're supposed to see her back home. But where's home? And if she's unconscious, how can we find out?"

"The patch on her jacket. What's Avenger Field?" I asked. "I've never heard of it!"

Akiko turned away from the pilot to face us both. "Mae had better figure that out fast," she said. "Because she's going to fly us there!"

Mae looked stunned.

"You're the only one who knows how to operate a plane!" Akiko exclaimed, pointing at Jane's wreck. "We've got to get this thing back home, along with the pilot!"

"Plus, Violet Vortex, you're full of facts," I said, urging her on. "Surely you've heard of the WASPs and where they come from. Is it California? Florida? Maine?"

If it were possible to look even more stunned, then Mae did. "I have no idea! I've never seen that patch on her jacket or the little pixie! And I've certainly never heard of a place called Avenger Park!"

"Avenger Field," corrected Akiko.

"Okay, *Avenger Field*! How am I supposed to fly us there?" she said, her voice climbing higher as if on its own flight. "And in a wrecked plane? I do all right in Aunt Willa's Piper Cub, but I'm best on the Link Trainer—pretending to fly! On the ground!"

She paused to catch her breath. But she seemed to want to keep Akiko from getting in another word. "Besides! There isn't even room in this plane! It's a single-seater. How are the three of us going to squeeze in?"

Akiko and I stared at each other for a beat or two. My hands felt sweaty inside my gloves. What in the world were we going to do?

"And you!" said Mae, rounding on me and forgetting all about her usual gentle, polite manners. "What are you talking about? Telling her we'll make sure her plane is all fixed up? Do you have a mechanic's license? Or are you thinking you'll just carry it on your shoulders over to Aunt Willa's hangar?"

Akiko smacked a hand to her forehead. She mumbled something about Infinity *Calamity*.

Sirens sounded in the distance, and I knew the fire department and police were on their way. We were in a pickle, and we'd have to figure out a plan. Fast.

"We've got lots of powers between us, right?" I said quickly, my words tumbling out. "I don't know if my healing power can work on objects, like this plane, or if it's just for living things. But I'm certainly willing to try.

"And Violet Vortex," I said, putting my hand on Mae's shoulder to steady her nerves, "you don't have to fly this plane. You're not the only one who can move us around. The Orange Inferno can get this pilot and her plane back home."

Akiko started to protest. "I can't exactly pull a tow truck out of my pouch—"

"By teleporting!" I interrupted. "Teleporting is the best way to get around. You remind us about it all the time."

"But something so heavy—"

"Emerald Shield is right," mumbled Mae. "ALL THE TIME."

"But where—"

"Who knows where, Orange Inferno?" I said, feeling panic bubbling up inside me like soda in a bottle. There was no more time for talking. We needed to disappear from downtown Chicago and be on our way to Jane's home base immediately. "We'll figure out the rest once we get there!"

Mae's eyes searched the sky again. "My aunts," she whispered.

Fire trucks and police cars were rounding the corner at the top of the block. We had only seconds to act. Turning back to Akiko and me, Mae signaled for us to grab hold of each other, Jane, and the airplane.

"Emerald Shield is right," she whispered urgently. "Just say we want to go to Avenger Field! Or *near* it! That should give us the time we need to sort ourselves out."

"Now, Orange Inferno!" I yelled as a fire truck barreled toward us. "Let's go!"

Fifteen

$\mathcal{M}$Y STOMACH DROPPED. BUT HAVING FLOWN in one of those small planes with Mae's aunt, I guess the feeling was getting a little familiar. Teleporting was like a plunge down a playground slide—with the added uncertainty of where exactly we'd land.

"Ouch!" I hollered, stumbling backward onto my bottom. "What is this place?"

I'd fallen onto some sort of rock or knotty bush. A dry wind was blowing, and I had to blink fast to keep the dust out of my eyes. As I looked around, I saw pale stones and scratchy shrubs stretching out in all directions. The sky looked bigger and wider than I'd ever seen in Philadelphia. It spread out above us in endless blue, from one side of the scrubby horizon to the other. There were no buildings or tall trees to block my view.

"The plane made it," said Mae in her usual sunny way. "And Jane did too! Thank goodness!"

"You sound surprised," said Akiko, letting out a few sneezes. "Did you think I wouldn't be able to get it right?"

Mae admitted she'd had some doubts. We all remembered the trip to my neighborhood bully's apartment in Philadelphia, where Akiko had first teleported us. I'd deposited stolen bikes right into Toby Hunter's bedroom, making sure his dad would catch him. But then Akiko had left me behind. While I was impressed with her superpowers, I wasn't 100 percent sure she could teleport with an airplane. Or that she'd remember to bring us along!

"Well, sometimes you're a little overconfident—"

"It's my turn now," I said, hoping to head off another back-and-forth debate between Akiko and Mae about who was the better superhero. "Step back, please. I'm hoping I can heal the bump on Jane's head before she wakes up. Then I'll focus on fixing up the damage to her plane."

I took a deep breath and gazed down at the wound above Jane's eyebrow. I reached for her shoulder.

"Wrong," Akiko corrected, not even bothering to whisper. "You'd better fix the plane first. We can't have Jane wake up, see we're the Infinity Trinity, and then watch us transform back into three regular kids. She'd know too much about us!"

"Orange Inferno is right," agreed Mae. "Restore the plane first."

I sighed. I think I liked it more when they were picking on each other!

"Okay, okay," I said. "But I don't want you giving me directions. Why don't you two walk around and figure out where we are?"

Akiko and Mae marched off, though Mae's purple cape caught on a tumbleweed or some sort of prickly bush. Akiko knelt to help her. I wanted to laugh as I watched them. They didn't exactly look heroic just then.

I turned to Jane—a pilot for the war effort. Like the mathematicians Jean Jennings and my cousin Kay McNulty, the code crackers Elizebeth Friedman and Genevieve Grotjan, and the spy Noor Khan, Jane and the other WASPs were using their human powers to fight bad guys. Maybe they were what real heroes looked like.

Jane had sounded worried about her plane. Would she be in trouble with the WASPs if it were damaged?

"Okay, plane," I whispered, "we'll get you looking good again. Then we'll deposit your pilot at Avenger Field and be on our way. We've got some bigger business to attend to."

I felt my heart start to race at the thought of what "bigger business" lay ahead for us. Like tracking down those spies who took Mae's aunts. Like finding a way to Paris. Like locating Zenobia and the other missing superheroes. Not to mention fighting Nazis and bringing everybody safely home. Once we'd done all that, then Mae might see her dad again, and Akiko might see her brother.

I tried to focus my mind. The bright sun was burning down on us, and as I touched the plane, it felt hot despite my gloves. I pressed both my hands to the wing, spreading my palms open. My cheeks grew warm beneath my mask as I took a deep breath and held it.

I thought about pilots like Jane and my dad, Aunt Willa and Aunt Janet, and everybody who was willing to step forward and do whatever they could to fight evil. There were so many people putting themselves at incredible risk in order to keep the rest of us safe.

"Emerald Shield," called a voice in a gravelly whisper. "You did it! The plane's all better. No more burnt patches!"

I snapped back to the moment and opened my eyes just in time to catch a glimpse of the cracked windshield sealing itself smooth and flat again. Wiping sweat from my forehead, I saw Akiko and Mae smiling over at me from the other side of the cockpit. And not only that, but Jane was starting to stir as well. Her cheeks had a bit of color to them now, and the welt over her right eye was gone.

"Look at the pilot!" whispered Mae, bouncing nervously

on her toes. "We can't return her to the base as we are, dressed as superheroes! We've got to transform, and fast! Come on—back to our regular-kid selves! Before she wakes up!"

As Jane was coming to, the three of us made the blink-of-an-eye switch from superhero costumes to ordinary clothes. Only now I wished I'd given thought to something other than my usual denim pants. I could use a broad-brimmed hat to keep my nose and cheeks from a sunburn. And with the heat so intense, a summer dress would be a lot cooler than heavy dungarees.

Mae and Akiko in their cotton skirts looked comfortable. I pulled my hair off my neck and fanned it, trying to cool my body temperature down. It was no use.

We crowded in on either side of Jane. Her brown hair was shoulder-length and curly, and her eyes were bright. She pushed her way out of the cockpit, and to our surprise, she wasn't much taller than we were.

"Where am I?" she asked. "And who are you?"

We told her we were near Avenger Field, though we didn't let on that we had no idea where exactly that was. Jane looked around at the dry and dusty landscape. Then she pointed over Mae's shoulder, at an arch on the horizon. It was like a metal rainbow.

"There's the gate," she said, grabbing her bag from the cockpit. "We're almost home!"

Sixteen

$\mathcal{J}$ANE SET OUT WALKING NORTH FROM THE
spot where we'd landed, cutting a trail through even more
pale rocks and prickly shrubs. The spiky bushes seemed to
reach out and grab my white socks as we followed after her.

"Do you kids live around here?" she asked, marching
ahead at a fast pace. "Is that how you found me?"

Akiko sneezed. Once, twice, three times. I figured the
dust we were kicking up was doing a number on her allergies and asthma. Though I knew the sneezing bothered
Akiko, it gave us time to come up with an answer for Jane.

"We're . . . not really from around here," Mae began.

"We noticed your plane going down," I added vaguely.

"We wanted to help if we could," finished Akiko, blowing her nose into a hankie from her Hauntima bag.

We nodded to each other as we scrambled along behind Jane. That answer would have to do. It wasn't exactly a lie. But it also didn't let her know we were superheroes who had teleported her and her airplane all the way from Chicago.

"I must have hit my head. I don't really recall what happened," Jane said. "I was flying over Chicago when I saw a storm or something—I can't remember. I'm just happy the plane seems okay. Those Mustangs are important fighter planes. We've got to get them to the troops who need them, so we can win this war."

I looked toward Akiko. Her face went serious, and I knew she must have been thinking about her brother. Mae nodded in agreement. She was probably thinking of her dad too. I squeezed my eyes shut, picturing my father in his plane over the Pacific. Had he flown a Mustang, like Jane's?

After we had been hiking behind Jane in the hot sun for what felt like hours, she finally called out. She was pointing up ahead, at a row of airplane hangars rising up from the dusty landscape like a desert oasis. Now that we were closer, I could better see the big metal arch we'd spotted earlier. It had lettering on it, though I wasn't able to read the words. The sun's glare was too intense. But what I could make out was a wooden sign that stood off to our right, as if guarding the gate, as we approached.

"Avenger Field," I said, barely getting the words out from my dry throat. "It says it right there, underneath that pixie on the sign."

The pixie looked just like the one on the patch sewn to Jane's leather jacket. She'd tossed the jacket over her shoulder in this heat. But I was close enough to be able to compare it to the one on the sign, and they matched exactly.

"We're protected by Fifinella herself," Jane explained. "She's the mascot of us WASPs. From the minute I arrived here in Sweetwater, Texas, I knew Fifinella was watching over all of us pilots. She helps us come back safely."

The pixie Fifinella smiled at us from the painted wooden sign. Curly yellow horns topped her head, long blue wings rose off her back, and tall boots reached her knees—just like we'd seen on the patch.

"Sweetwater, Texas?" Akiko raised her eyebrows, and Mae shot me a knowing smile. Now we had the answer to where we were! Avenger Field was located in the dry, dusty, treeless, tumbleweed-loving Texas town of Sweetwater!

"Come on in, and I'll introduce you around," Jane said in an easy, welcoming manner. She seemed so calm as to be unflappable. If I were ever to go up in a plane again, I'd want to be flying with Jane. She had a way about her that showed she'd stay calm no matter what sort of chaos was happening around her.

Just as we stepped through the gate, Mae lost her footing and stumbled into Akiko's side. Suddenly dizzy, she winced like she had a piercing headache. Akiko put her arm around Mae to steady her.

"My head," she said, pressing her temples. "It hurts."

"It's not him again, is it?" whispered Akiko. "The Metallic Falcon? Do you think he can read your mind?"

Mae shook her head as if she were trying to clear away any bad thoughts.

"Don't let him!" I pressed my mouth to her ear, speaking softly but with a frantic urgency. "Don't think of Fifinella or even the words on that sign. Don't give the Metallic Falcon any clues to where we are!"

"You're not the Violet Vortex right now," said Akiko, her voice frightened. "He shouldn't have a clear connection."

"Right," I agreed, "but Nova said he's incredibly powerful."

Mae turned her eyes to me. She looked more scared than I'd ever seen her.

"I'm trying. But it may be too late," she whispered, pinching her eyes shut. "It felt like he was there—the same as when I was the Violet Vortex in Chicago."

Jane was almost to the first building. A few women

wearing oversize jumpsuits were walking toward her. We needed to catch up without drawing too much suspicion about what we were doing here.

"Let's meet these pilots," Akiko whispered, taking Mae by the other elbow as the three of us shuffled along the rocky path. "We've got to get our story straight on how we returned Jane and her Mustang plane. Then we've got to figure out how to get out of here!"

"And how to get to Paris," I whispered. "Zenobia and the others need us. Now!"

"And don't forget Aunt Willa and Aunt Janet," Mae said softly, pushing a few hairs away from her forehead and straightening her shoulders. "There are a lot of people counting on us. This is no time for mistakes!"

Seventeen

"WHERE'D YOU KIDS COME FROM?" ASKED one of the women. She was cuffing the sleeves of a jumpsuit that seemed much too large. The pant legs were rolled up too. I noticed that most of the women walking by in the busy hubbub were wearing similar outfits. "We don't get too many children here."

Akiko gulped. Mae took a slight step backward.

They were leaving me to do the talking this time.

"We were just . . . ah . . . p-passing through," I stammered. "Kind of stumbled into Jane here."

Jane explained about her Mustang and how she must

have hit her head. "But I feel fit as a fiddle now," she said. "And even though I had to bring that Mustang down in a field over there, I nailed the landing. The plane's okay."

I could see aircraft of all sizes and colors parked in the hangars and on the tarmac around us. A crew was sent out to load Jane's plane onto a truck and bring it back to the mechanics for inspection. I hoped that would be the end of our having to explain. Maybe we could teleport out of here before we were pressed on it again. I didn't want Jane to get into any trouble. But I also didn't want too much poking around about how the three of us had shown up here, in what seemed to be the middle of nowhere!

"What exactly do WASPs do?" asked Akiko, thankfully firing off a question so fast that the pilots didn't have time to interrogate us. "Can you perform spirals and loops? Are you allowed to fly all those planes? Do the men let you?"

Jane said they spent about twelve hours each day on the airfield, learning about the different planes and flight procedures and how to navigate through the sky when they lost radio contact. "Half the day, we're up in the air flying. The other half, we're studying how engines work and what to do when the weather changes."

Another pilot, this one tall with yellowish hair, held a hankie to her nose as the wind kicked up. Akiko let out another sneeze, then reached into her bag for her own hankie. "The dust here is terrible," said the pilot. "It gets into your teeth, your hair, your eyes."

"I don't know which tastes worse—the dust or the food," said Jane with a smile. "We eat green beans for breakfast, green beans for lunch, and green beans for dinner."

"The green beans are bad," said a third pilot with an easy laugh, "but the scorpions are worse. They get in your boots. And don't get me started on the rattlesnakes!"

Mae, Akiko, and I shuddered. Green beans and dust and scorpions were bad enough. But snakes? Ever since the Hisser in Philadelphia, none of us could bear any mention of slithery serpents.

"I'm heading for the classroom," said the third pilot, and she pointed toward a one-story building across the way. "I'm picking up a plane in Oklahoma, then delivering it to California. I've got to go over the maps, and after that I've got to calculate what speed and altitude will be best, factoring in the wind and weather and all that."

"Just like Jean Jennings and Cousin Kay," whispered Mae, "the way they calculate how the wind and weather influence where the bombs hit the enemy."

Jane overheard us. She asked who Jean and Kay were.

"They're some other smart people we know," I said, trying not to reveal too much. The ENIAC project was top secret. Nobody was supposed to know about it.

Mae began asking questions too. She must have been

thinking about her aunts Willa and Janet. "How old were you when you learned to fly?" she asked in her polite way. "What made you want to start?"

Jane watched a bright yellow plane take off down a runway on the other side of the low classroom building. Then she turned back to us. "One of my teachers told me about a pilot training program. For every nine men who enrolled, they would let in one woman. I decided to give it a try."

She cupped her hand to her eyes and followed the yellow plane as it climbed higher into the cloudless blue sky. "The first time I ever flew, I thought I was an angel looking down at the earth," she said. "I loved it. And I couldn't wait to get back up again."

"Same with me," said Akiko, her voice sounding a little awestruck. "It's an incredible feeling being up there—"

"We *imagine* it's incredible," I said, nudging Akiko with my shoe. She was going to get us in trouble. "It's not like we have much experience flying or anything."

"I've got a brother in the navy," Jane said, nodding for us to come with her. "And my sister joined the Red Cross. When I got the telegram inviting me to come here to Sweetwater to join the WASPs, my teachers tried to talk me out of it. But I told them I knew exactly how I could do my part for the war.

"I would fly."

Akiko ignored my nudge and went on chatting. She

told Jane about her brother, Tommy, fighting with the 442nd Regimental Combat Team, and about Mae's daddy and mine. How the three of us just wanted to do our part to help fight too.

"Like the heroes in our comic books," she went on, pulling a copy of Nova the Sunchaser from her bag and showing it to Jane. "Josie, Mae, and I want to be like Nova, Hopscotch, and Hauntima. And Zenobia; her sister, the Palomino; and her sidekick, Star. We want to fight evil everywhere."

Jane stood still and read a few pages, squinting in the glare of the unforgiving sun. I could see the heat rising in waves off the hot tarmac.

"You kids remind me of myself," she said. "The moment I saw the cover of *LIFE* magazine with a woman pilot on it—she was about my age, hair in two braids, sitting on the wing of a plane—I thought, *This is what I really want to do.*

"Sometimes we have to see it before we can be it."

Jane set out across the open courtyard of the busy compound, and we raced along behind her to keep up. We heard shouts coming from pilots near the runway, trying to be heard over the roar of planes' propellers. Another cluster of pilots sat at a picnic table, reading thick manuals and writing in notebooks. Once we reached the welcome shade of one of the enormous airplane hangars, we saw that even more pilots were inside, standing around a table and taking apart an engine.

"That group over there is learning to work the radios," Jane said, pointing toward a row of wooden tables. "We have to master Morse code, since we navigate by radio signals from towers across the country. Got to understand radio messages, no mistakes."

"Us too," exclaimed Mae.

I smacked my forehead. These two were going to get us caught!

"What Mae means," I said, shooting her a look, "is that we mess around with radios too. It's good to know the latest technology."

I must have sounded pretty stiff. But what else was I supposed to do? With Akiko and Mae leaking information like spaghetti strainers? I had a hundred questions for Jane and the other WASPs too. But we needed to turn our attention to getting in touch with Mrs. B and figuring out a plan for Paris. Zenobia couldn't wait much longer.

I watched Jane fold up her helmet and goggles, then hang her pilot's jacket on a hook. She reminded me of Aunt Willa and Aunt Janet. Surely they couldn't wait much longer either.

Eighteen

"LISTEN UP, PILOTS!" CALLED A SHARP VOICE
from the other side of the hangar. "We've got the boss coming in a couple minutes to talk about a big mission. So finish what you're doing, then gather round! She doesn't have
time to wait on any slowpokes!"

The pilot who'd done the yelling hopped down from
the chair she was standing on and walked over to a group
of other trainees. Most of them were in those same oversize jumpsuits we'd seen earlier. Jane said the training gear
came only in men's sizes, which was why most of the women
had to roll up the legs and arms to make them fit. Others

wore blue pants and pale-blue dress shirts like Jane's. She called this their flight uniform, but I couldn't believe they were allowed to wear slacks—hardly any women I knew wore pants! They did have blue skirts, Jane whispered, but WASPs wore them only for official events.

"Who's this boss she's talking about?" I asked as we walked toward the speaker's circle. "And what do you think the big mission is going to be about?"

"Jackie Cochran, the pilot who started the WASPs," Jane explained. And patting the silver pin on her shirt, she added, "Jackie does it all. She even paid for our wings out of her own wallet."

Suddenly the hangar fell quiet as a tallish woman walked in from the building next door. I stood on my tiptoes for a better look. Her hair was smoothed back, and her cropped jacket was the same blue as the other uniforms. She smiled easily, and I couldn't help but notice she was wearing the brightest red lipstick I'd ever seen.

"She got her start running a makeup company," whispered Jane, as if she'd read my mind. "Jackie's got style by the bucketload."

I listened as Jackie Cochran greeted the pilots and talked about the different kinds of aircraft coming and going across the country. Her words faded in and out as I looked around at all the pilots. Learning to fly with a cape had been fairly easy. I wondered if I could ever get the hang of how to handle an airplane. Maybe Jane could teach me how to read all those dials on the dashboard, and how to take off and land. Or maybe Mae could do it. Or her aunts—

"We leave for London this evening."

I snapped to attention.

"What did she just say?" I squeaked, turning to Jane. "Who's going to London?"

Jane laughed and patted my shoulder. She said something about Jackie having a plan for one of the important planes. She was looking for volunteers. "I think I'll put my name in," Jane said. She was confident without being showy. "I'd like to see London. I'll bet there aren't scorpions or rattlesnakes there."

London? I tried to picture it on a map, on the other side of the Atlantic Ocean. It wasn't all the way to Paris, where Zenobia and the others were. But it was a lot closer than we were right now!

"Come on, Josie," said Jane, heading back, "we've lost your friends. Let's find them and see if we can't introduce you kids around."

I'd been so excited to see all the women pilots, I hadn't even noticed that Mae and Akiko weren't with us. The mess hall was the most likely place Akiko would wander. Or maybe Mae had led them over to one of the flight trainers. I pictured her sitting inside at the controls, just like she'd done in her aunts' hangar back in Chicago.

I trailed behind Jane, weaving right and left, past pilots and mechanics and what must have been teachers. The hangar was so loud now from all the excited talking and engines roaring just outside, I could hardly think.

"There you are," called Jane as we spotted Akiko and Mae. They were standing near the row of radios, and their expressions were tense. "It's about time for my class on radio transmissions and Morse code. When it's done, why don't you all join us for supper in the mess hall. But after that, you kids will have to head home. There's a phone in the office to call your parents."

Mae seemed to be forcing a polite smile, but I could tell she was too worked up to speak. Akiko's cheeks were flushed, and her breathing was louder than usual. It might have been allergies from the dusty wind, though I suspected something more was going on with the two of them.

"We'll sit in the back," Akiko volunteered, grabbing my arm and dragging me toward the farthest row of desks. Other WASPs filed past us, their eyebrows raised. I heard Jane explain that we were interested in radios and planes too. So they smiled and seemed to be all right about letting three kids sit in on their lesson.

"We've got a message," began Akiko, trying to whisper, even before we'd slipped into our seats. She plunged her hand into her bag and pulled out pencils and paper. "We haven't solved it. But we think it's him. Hauntima's ghost, we *know* it's him!"

I whispered for her to slow down. And to lower her voice. But I knew that might be impossible.

"Who?" I asked. "Are you talking about the Metallic Falcon?"

Just saying his name made my heartbeat quicken. Worry flooded my veins.

"Yes. We pulled on a headset and listened to the radio when you walked off with Jane," said Mae. She spoke so low, I had to lean in closer to hear. "We tried the frequencies we'd used in San Francisco. You know, the ones where we heard Side-Splitter's voice. There was nothing but static for a while, but then—"

"Then we heard this tapping," interrupted Akiko. "I wrote it down, you know, just out of habit. And look what it says!"

STAIRSTEP

OPTION WARS

Without hesitating, I grabbed a pencil and began scribbling across the page. Akiko and Mae did too. We'd seen enough by now to know it was a coded message. But what was it telling us? Scrambling and unscrambling the letters, we tried to form new words and solve it—quickly. So much was at stake.

To Jane and the other WASPs in the desks around us, we must have looked like eager students. Heads down, pencils moving, focus intense. But in our minds, we were desperate!

"In the first clue, I see 'pest,' 'test,' 'rest,'" whispered Mae, rearranging the letters.

"I see 'paste,' 'taste,'" Akiko said hoarsely. "'Strap, trap'—"

"Trap?" I nearly shouted. "I see it too."

The three of us paused, staring at the message and then into one another's faces.

"And if we mark out those letters, T-R-A-P," said Mae, "what's left?"

"I can spell 'set,'" said Akiko. Her jaw clenched.

"That's it," I said, not wanting to speak the words. "When we unscramble STAIRSTEP, here's what it spells."

TRAP IS SET

As we moved to the next line, I knew exactly what clue waited for us. It was the most important city for the league of secret heroes right now. And we needed to get there as fast as we could: *Paris.*

"The next words, *OPTION WARS*," Mae said, her voice steely instead of scared. "Strike through P-A-R-I-S, and what's left?"

Without slowing down, Akiko wrote the answer out in bold block letters.

TRAP IS SET
NOW TO PARIS

Nineteen

WE SAT IN SILENCE AS THE MEANING OF THE message sank in. There was no doubting what it was about. Zenobia and the other superheroes were in Paris, trapped and powerless at the Eiffel Tower. And now it was clear that someone was on their way, probably to finish them off!

"It's got to be the Metallic Falcon," Mae said, her voice catching. "We've got to get there before him!"

"But we can't teleport into Nazi territory," Akiko said a little too loudly. Some of the pilots shushed us. I scooted closer to Akiko's desk so we could whisper. "What if we landed right in front of some armed guards or something? Or on a land mine? It's too dangerous!"

I sat still for a moment more, staring out at the tarmac and the planes. What if we caught a ride overseas? It would be dangerous, that was certain. But what else could we do? So many people were living in danger every single day. I closed my eyes and imagined my father in his plane over the Pacific Ocean. I would do anything to keep the rest of our family safe—my mom, my little brothers, my cousin.

"We can stow away in a plane," I whispered, looking around to make sure none of the WASPs were listening. "I heard the lady in charge—Jackie Cochran—tell everyone about a special mission. They're taking one of the fancy planes across the Atlantic. All the way to London!"

Akiko shook her head.

"London is in England, Josie," she said with what might have been an eye roll. "That's not exactly Paris—"

"It's close enough," interrupted Mae. "You're right that we can't teleport there, Akiko. And while our superpowers are strong, we can't fly that far, either. It would be exhausting. So Josie's idea of letting an airplane carry us is a good one. It's the best we've got."

The instructor walked past our desks as he talked about radio towers and the language of piloting. We pretended to pay attention to the chalkboard and take notes on his lecture. But once he passed, we began whispering again.

"Nova says the Metallic Falcon is one of the most powerful supervillains ever," Akiko whispered. "He turned those birds into metal statues. And the planes and pilots too! What will happen once he gets to the Eiffel Tower? What will he do to Zenobia and the other superheroes?"

I flinched at the thought. Mae shuddered like a cold draft blew over her.

"He's definitely scary," I said. "And dangerous. Which means we can't let Mrs. B and Astra know about this fight. It would destroy them."

We sat quietly as the WASPs around us took notes in their books and asked questions of the instructor. There was so much to think about, so many innocent lives at stake.

"This battle is ours," Mae said finally. "Josie's right. We'll have to leave Room Twelve out of it."

"I can't bear the thought of losing Mrs. B," Akiko said softly. And her voice fell as she added, "Or Astra."

Around us the WASPs began getting to their feet and collecting their notebooks from their desks. The lesson must have ended, though the three of us didn't exactly notice. Jane walked over to where we were seated, and she had two friends with her. They were the same two pilots we'd met on our arrival—the tall one with the hankie and the short one with the easy laugh.

"It's time for supper now," Jane said, pointing toward what must have been the mess hall. "You girls can join us. But then you'll have to get moving before lights-out. They're sticklers for rules around here."

We thanked her for showing us around. She and the other WASPs could have stopped us at the gate. Instead they welcomed us like we were little sisters. I made sure to let them know we'd leave before the first stars came out.

But with a wink from Akiko, the three of us silently committed to our plan. We would stow away on Jackie Cochran's fancy plane and be on our way to London while the rest of Avenger Field slept.

Twenty

"OUCH, MOVE YOUR FOOT," I WHISPERED. "You're smashing my fingers!"

"Keep it down or they'll hear us," Mae warned. "And that means you, too, Akiko."

Even though I could barely see in the darkness at the back of the plane, I knew exactly where Akiko was. Her raspy breathing was just beside my left ear, so close that with every exhale, she blew a lock of my hair against my cheek. It tickled.

"Shhhh," I said. "Sounds like they're right outside."

Voices drifted through the plane's open door. They

must have been the mechanics, since their questions were all about gas lines and spark plugs and rudders.

Next we heard people climbing on board, and I held my breath so as to not make a single noise. Akiko and Mae were doing the same, I assumed, since the storage area where we were hiding went completely silent.

"Get comfortable, everyone," someone said. "We're in for a long ride."

I recognized that voice! It was Jane's! I bit my knuckle to keep from exclaiming. I couldn't see Akiko's or Mae's expressions in the dark. But I knew they were probably as excited by her presence as I was.

"We'll stop in Newfoundland on the eastern edge of Canada, then again in Greenland and Iceland," said another voice. I knew right away it belonged to Jackie Cochran. I'd have to tell Mae and Akiko about her later, since they had been listening to the radio when she spoke to all the pilots. "Then we'll sweep into England, arriving in London before we know it."

I wasn't sure who else had climbed onto the plane with Jane and Jackie. But there must have been two or three others. Judging by the sound of them moving around, I figured they had taken seats about a car's length away from us. Now they were quiet as Jane went through the final review before takeoff.

"Oil level, check. Visibility, check."

Once she'd gone through her list, we heard the propellers roar to life. Moments later, I could feel a sense of motion as the plane began to roll.

We picked up speed, and a hand in the darkness grabbed my right arm and squeezed. It was Mae. I reached to my left and took hold of Akiko's hand. We may have been stowaways hiding in a storage area, but we were on our way to help fight this war.

Tense and alert, we clutched one another's hands in the pitch black as Jane steered the plane faster and faster down the runway. The engine whirred, filling our ears with a noisy hum. Finally, we lifted off the ground and into the night sky.

In silence, Mae, Akiko, and I stared up at the nearby window at the stars beyond. We'd been flying for what could have been a half hour—I had no idea how to measure time in the darkness—when I started to shiver from the chill. Up so high in the nighttime clouds, the temperature was much colder than on the ground in the Texas heat. I wished for a blanket.

Cupping my hands around Mae's ear so she could hear me over the noise, I asked her if she could feel anything nearby. Moments later she produced a scratchy piece of material and draped it over my legs. It was big enough to cover her and Akiko too.

"Long trip," I called to the two of them over the engine's roar. "Sleep!"

The three of us curled up, resting heads and arms and feet together as we nestled into the knapsacks and bags that had been stowed around us. I wasn't even worried about Akiko snoring. With the growl of the plane's propellers, we would be safe from discovery all the way until sunrise. There was no way anybody up front would be able to hear us. And in the heavy darkness, nobody would see us either.

We slept hard, waking only vaguely on what must have been the stops for fueling up. Hours later—or judging by our hungry stomachs, maybe a whole day—the plane bounced back to earth with a particularly bumpy landing. The sun was rising, I guessed, because the light had grown coral colored inside our plane. The wheels tapped out a rhythm as we taxied along the runway. I tried to picture what it looked like outside the row of windows. Was this England?

Jackie Cochran unfastened her harness and left the pilots' seats. Peeking out from under the blanket, I tried to catch a glimpse of the other travelers she was speaking to in the rows ahead of us. But no matter how much I craned my neck, they remained just out of view.

"Thanks to Jane's excellent flying, we've made a safe landing," Jackie began. "We'll have much to do starting the moment we step outside. The Nazis have blitzed London with ferocious bombing attacks, and the damage to buildings and streets is painful to see. While the English are strong, they need our help."

Jane left her seat at the controls and came to stand beside Jackie. Her expression was serious as she folded her aviator's helmet in her hands. It made me think of Aunt Willa and Aunt Janet.

That's why we were here—to help those too powerless to fight.

I thought about Astra and how weak he'd gotten in San Francisco. Mrs. B too. When they were without their moonstone collar and ring, they'd seemed as if they might fade into mist. Those moonstones came from the Masked Moonflower, who drew her power from the moon. She'd passed along special powers to her children, Zenobia and the Palomino, in the form of the moonstones. Astra too.

Without them, they were powerless.

Thank goodness we had Zenobia's moonstone in the Hauntima bag. Once Zenobia slipped it onto her finger again, we hoped her power would be restored. Maybe the powers of all the superheroes would be restored, and this awful war could end. And more innocent people wouldn't have to suffer.

I closed my eyes, and Baby Lou and Vinnie came to mind. I wondered how they were doing without me home to tell them bedtime stories and share stacks of comic books. My little brothers might not have been listening to bombs falling and bullets flying, but they were still suffering. They missed our dad with all their hearts, and knowing he was gone forever . . . It was a lot for a little kid to take.

I could feel Mae and Akiko on either side of me. With all the worry they felt for their dad and brother, they were suffering too.

". . . believe it's time we discuss the details of this plan of attack," Jackie was saying, her voice clear and confident. "It's more important than ever that we defeat this enemy, once and for all. Don't you agree, Josie, Akiko, and Mae?"

What?

Was I hearing things?

Had she just spoken our names?

My heart seemed to stop midbeat. And Mae and Akiko, who seconds ago had been peeking out from under the blanket, yanked it over their heads to hide. I clutched my section to my nose.

We must have misheard her. How could Jackie Cochran know about us? And what about Jane? We couldn't possibly involve the WASPs in our fight. It was much too dangerous to have them risk their lives in a battle against a supervillain!

"She's right, children," came another voice. "Now is the time we talk about what lies ahead. For all of us."

I recognized the voice, but I simply could not believe my ears. Again I craned my neck to get a glimpse of who the mysterious passengers were in the rows up ahead. Then, as she moved into a pale shaft of morning sunlight, I saw a face I recognized.

Mrs. B!

And leaping onto the plane's floor with a thud and bounding over to us was the only sidekick we could imagine just then. He wagged his furry tail and licked our faces in between barks and whimpers and excited growls.

We couldn't keep from shouting. "Astra!"

Twenty-One

$\mathcal{M}$RS. B! ASTRA! WHAT ARE YOU DOING HERE?" croaked Akiko as we made our way up to the bench across from her, Jackie, and Jane. "How did you know?"

"How did we *not* know?" answered Mrs. B patiently. "In the league of secret heroes, it is our job to stay informed."

I was torn as I settled onto the bench, in between Akiko and Mae. One part of me was relieved to see her and know that Room Twelve was with us still, so far from home. But the other part of me worried for her safety, and Astra's, too. Even though they had their moonstones again, they seemed fragile. Much too fragile for a battle with a maniac like this metal bird.

"W-we can't let you fight, Mrs. B," I said, my voice shaky. "The Metallic Falcon could destroy you."

"We have to do this alone," agreed Akiko, as scratchy as sandpaper. "We can't risk anyone else. You're much too important."

Mae's voice was steady and strong as she turned to Jane and Jackie.

"That goes for you, too," she began. "The Metallic Falcon is dangerous. He's already kidnapped two pilots. We can't let him have any more."

Mrs. B got to her feet and, with help from Jane and Jackie, unfolded a small wooden table from a side panel. We gathered around as Mrs. B spread out a map.

"None of us knows what is ahead. But you can see that our league of secret heroes has many who are loyal," she said. "We draw on the talents of the best, brightest, and bravest. They make us proud every day."

Jane and Jackie nodded in thanks, but their expressions were serious.

Running a finger across the map, from London over the English Channel into France, Mrs. B stopped at Paris. "Here is what we know at this point: The messages have been coming from the Eiffel Tower. The Metallic Falcon is racing to get there. And, as you know, he threatens your very existence.

"And as superheroes, you've come to understand an important secret to power: taking your individual gifts and joining them. Together. That is how we rise above evil.

"Not alone in the battle. *Together*."

Voices from the airfield rose and fell outside our plane. But for the moment, each of us stood silent in our thoughts. I imagined our battles with the Hisser and Side-Splitter. Sure, we each had amazing powers—I loved my super-strength, and I admired Mae's ability to talk to animals and Akiko's power to shape-shift. But Mrs. B was right. We'd beaten them when we used these strengths as one. Together.

"Now," she continued after a deep breath, "no matter who you're up against—the Hisser, Side-Splitter, or any sinister force for ill—everyone has a weak spot." And on top of the map, Mrs. B unfurled a sort of blueprint of the Metallic Falcon, with notes and comments marking his wings and beak and eyes. "But before we discuss his, I must make something clear to you."

She smoothed the blueprint slowly with both her hands. "None of us is ever truly alone in the fight. Even if no one is standing by our side, even if we feel completely abandoned, the people we love travel with us. They are the flames that light our way. They are the fires that burn inside us. They are the stars that inspire us to shine brighter.

"The league of secret heroes will not let you out of our sights," Mrs. B said in a voice tight with concern. "We have operatives positioned in the air, on the land, in the sea.

So long as the Violet Vortex, the Orange Inferno, and the Emerald Shield are in the fight, we will be too."

Suddenly a siren pierced the air. The blast made me jump. Akiko and Mae grabbed my arms, and together we rushed from the plane. Jane, Jackie, and the others followed right behind. Crews were racing toward their aircraft, shouting about German bombers on the horizon.

"We've got to help," hollered Mae, thrusting her right hand forward.

"Now," answered Akiko. And she grabbed Mae's fist with her own.

"Let's go," I called, forcing a shaky voice from my throat. There was no time for fear. With a glance at Astra and Mrs. B, I reminded myself what we were fighting for. And *who*.

I wrapped my hand around Akiko's and Mae's. And a moment later, golden light burst into the air. Swirling streams of purple, orange, and green enveloped us like a funnel cloud and, transformed, we shot into the air.

Flying as the Infinity Trinity once again, we soared over the airport. I studied the field below us, trying to get a sense of how many planes could take off to meet those Nazis. Pilots were already lining up their aircraft along three different runways, and the sky was quickly filling with metal wings and roaring engines.

Where did we fit in? Should we charge straight into battle with the planes? Or would it be better to protect everyday citizens on the ground from the Nazi bombers? Before the three of us could work it out, I spotted something unusual in the sky not far from us.

"What is that?" I shouted.

Akiko pointed at a bright blur of red and blue shooting off to the left. And from the opposite direction came another shape, this one red and gold.

"Those definitely are *not* planes," warned Mae.

Now the two shapes buzzed side by side just above us.

"They're superheroes!" I yelled, nearly getting tangled up in my cape. "And judging by the size of them, they're kids!"

Twenty-Two

THE TWO FIGURES LOOPED AND CORK-screwed through the air, excitedly keeping pace beside us. I tried to concentrate on flying straight, but they were distracting. Mae and Akiko seemed thrown off too.

"Hauntima's ghost," exclaimed Akiko. "These two are a couple of show-offs!"

"Where did you come from?" called the red-and-blue one. Her accent sounded French to me. "We thought we were the only ones left! *Fantastique!*"

"What she means to say," said the other, her words seeming very British, "is you're a sight for sore eyes. We could use your help!"

"We're the Infinity Trinity," announced Akiko. "And we're ready to fight! Who are you?"

"I am called the Parisian Light," said the French one, her jet pack humming as she spiraled in the cloudy sky. "And my friend here with those big wings, she's the Golden Lion. Some call her the pride of Great Britain. Together we're doing the best we can, but all the superheroes we know have vanished!"

We seemed to be approaching a city now, flying above buildings and a wide river. As we rounded a bend over the water, I noticed a beautiful tower up ahead of us. It seemed tall enough to touch the gray clouds, tapering off to a delicate point. With its enormous round clockface, it stood out against the surrounding buildings. Most of them were much shorter, and many were bombed out.

"That clock must be Big Ben," hollered Mae. Like me, she'd probably seen enough newsreels at the theater to recognize its graceful shape. "We're flying over London, aren't we? I can't believe it!"

Akiko called over to our new superhero friends, explaining about Zenobia's messages from Paris and how we wanted to reach the Eiffel Tower as soon as we could. That was where we believed the missing superheroes were being held. That was where we needed to focus all of our energy.

"Ouch!" Mae cried suddenly, pressing a hand to her temple. "It's my head again!"

"No, Violet Vortex," I warned. "Don't let him read your mind! Block him!"

We slowed our flying until we were hovering in place high above the river. Akiko and I stayed close to Mae, making sure she didn't fall from the sky. The Parisian Light and the Golden Lion circled us protectively. "Are you okay?" they asked.

"It's . . . the Metallic Falcon," said Mae, her words halting. "He's trying . . . to get into my head!"

"The Emerald Shield is right," Akiko said. "Clear your mind. Or he'll figure out where we are. He'll know we're not in America anymore—that we're getting closer to Paris."

Mae pressed her hands to her temples and squeezed her eyes shut.

"I'm trying, Orange Inferno," she said. "It's so hard. He's stronger than I am."

"Don't give up," I told her, holding tight to her shoulder. "You can do this. Focus on beating him. Think about getting into his mind again. Use his power against him!"

Mae winced. Her headache must have been splitting as she tried to block his powers. Keeping her eyes shut tight, she took a deep breath.

"That's right," Akiko said. "Like Mrs. B said, everyone has a weak spot. Maybe the Metallic Falcon, despite all his powers, can't stop you from reading his mind!"

Mae rubbed at her temples again and breathed deeply.

"I can see what he's seeing, I think," she said, her voice a little shaky. "There's water, lots of water. Like he's flying over a lake. Or maybe it's a river. And it's really gray—the sky and the water."

"That could be anywhere," called the Parisian Light as she circled just above us. "This falcon, he could be crossing the Atlantic Ocean. He could be over the English Channel, trying to get to France."

Mae nodded, pressing on her temples and trying to keep her focus.

"There's something ahead of him," she said. "Dark, like birds . . . big birds."

Suddenly a hum in the distance caught my attention. It was low and droning. It carried on the wind not only to my ears, but to Akiko's, too. She whipped around and fixed her eyes on the southern horizon.

"He sees birds?" asked the Golden Lion, swooping in and hovering closer to Akiko and me. I could feel the rush of air from her beating wings. "Dark birds?"

The Parisian Light made her way nearer too. She joined us as we stared into the southern sky. Dark shapes, larger now than before, hung low on the horizon and moved steadily toward us. They looked frightening. Deadly.

And then, without warning, a single enormous bird rose into the air from the center of the flock. Its screeching call made me plug my ears and sent an icy chill through my veins.

"Those aren't birds," shouted the Parisian Light. "They're German bombers!"

"And he's with them!" I hollered breathlessly. "The Metallic Falcon—he's coming!"

Mae spun around, opening her eyes and trying to focus. She looked east and west, desperate to get her bearings. She gazed down on the far side of the river, where blocks and blocks of damaged buildings stood, the result of the Germans' bombing campaign. Then she turned to the opposite side, at Big Ben's enormous clockface.

"Again," she said, wincing from the pain at her temples. "He's doing it again—reading my mind."

"Don't let him see anything," Akiko said, reaching a hand out to reassure Mae. "He can't get to us if he doesn't know where we are!"

Twenty-Four

WE RAN AS FAST AS WE COULD. ALL AROUND us, air-raid sirens blared and more bombs fell. There was no time to follow the battle in the sky. We had to keep our heads down as we looked for shelter. Diving down side streets and keeping clear of bicycle riders whizzing past, we managed to avoid the rubble falling from brick buildings along our route.

A few blocks away, we saw a throng of people rushing toward an entrance for the underground train station. We joined them, eager to get below ground fast before German bombers struck again. But our pace slowed suddenly, and looking ahead, I realized there were crowds of other Londoners trying to do the same thing.

"Look at all these people," whispered Mae, holding tight to Akiko's arm and my shoulder. None of us wanted to get lost in this crush of men, women, and children hurrying to safety. "There must be hundreds. Can we all fit?"

"People everywhere," whispered Akiko, on her tiptoes to see the scene ahead of us. "I can hardly believe it."

Once we made it below, I was stunned to see Londoners sitting in every available space. Not only had they filled the train platform, but they covered the train tracks, too. And with the escalators out of service, people had taken seats up and down the unmoving stairs. In fact, grandparents and grown-ups, even kids, seemed to be everywhere we looked. As we walked deeper into the tunnel, we had to pick our way slowly so we didn't accidentally step on anyone's fingers.

"This looks promising," I called over my shoulder to Mae and Akiko. I was following a pair of mothers who were marching their six or seven kids toward an open patch of track farther down the line, to our left. "I think I see a vacant spot."

We sat down just a foot or so away from one of the children—a little boy about five years old. He reminded me of Baby Lou and Vinnie, and I felt a pang of homesickness. I wondered if they were safe back in Philadelphia. At least

America wasn't being bombed the way London was.

Akiko, Mae, and I looked around in silence. I could hardly believe my eyes. While I knew everyone underground here must have been terrified, not many people were letting on. Voices were calm as people reassured one another that the attack would pass, eventually.

How could the English be so brave?

With each new explosion, the walls shook and the shelter fell quiet. Every ear must have been listening for the planes, every mind imagining what the street above us would look like when we emerged. I wondered whether any of the shops or office buildings we'd passed would still be standing.

"That was a close call out there on the bridge," Mae said in a serious whisper. "Too close!"

"Are we safe down here in the subway?" croaked Akiko, looking around again. "What if the Metallic Falcon comes underground looking for us?"

I stared at my hands and feet as I turned this thought around and around in my head. My gloves and boots were gone, as were my cape, mask—the whole costume. The whole Emerald Shield. What were Akiko, Mae, and I now? Were we superheroes anymore?

"There's a chance the Metallic Falcon will be able to find us," I said slowly, my stomach beginning to knot. "His powers of telepathy are strong. Remember when we first reached Avenger Field in Texas? He seemed to be trying to read Mae's mind then. That could be how he tracked us here."

Mae shook her head. "No way. He can't find us down here—I won't let him. When our superpowers disappeared up on the bridge, the connection broke between his mind and mine. He may be able to read the Violet Vortex's thoughts. But he can't read Mae Crumpler's."

Akiko looked confused. "You think losing our powers is a good thing?" she asked. But then she answered her own question. "It's not! We're doomed without them. We can't teleport. We can't shape-shift. We can't—"

"Stop thinking about what we can't do," interrupted Mae. "Let's talk about what we *can* do."

We fell quiet. I watched some kids near us play a game of cards. The sounds of more explosions on the streets above blended with the quiet conversations of children, parents, and grandparents up and down the tracks. What in the world were we going to do now? We'd come all this way in order to save Zenobia and the other superheroes trapped in Paris. But what good were we without powers?

Powerless.

There was that word again. We'd read it in one of the secret messages sent by Zenobia, calling for help. Without her moonstone ring, she was as weak as Mrs. B and Astra had been.

"Okay, let's focus on the things we're good at," Mae said, trying to stay positive.

"Great," said Akiko with an eye roll. "We'll make friends with all of London's dogs and cats. And we'll give them cute names like Pippa and Nigel—"

"Seriously, Akiko," I interrupted. "We are good at lots of things. Think about our puzzling skills. All three of us are great at cracking secret messages."

Suddenly Akiko seemed to remember something. She opened her Hauntima bag and began rooting around inside. I imagined what was in there: sunglasses, shoes, somehow an umbrella. I bet if I wanted a pogo stick, she could find that in her bag too. When she pulled her hand out, I saw two chocolate bars and a small slip of paper.

"I wish this were an apple pie," she said. "I'd even eat a blueberry or a cherry one if it were possible." It had been so long since the mess-hall dinner at Avenger Field, my stomach growled at the thought.

Akiko passed one of the chocolate bars to Mae and me to open. Then she turned to the little boy beside us and tried handing him a chocolate bar too. He stared at it with a look of amazement, as if Akiko were a magician. Silently he looked up at her; then he took the chocolate bar from her palm and turned to his sisters.

"That was so nice," whispered Mae in obvious surprise. "You are a constant source of wonder, Akiko!"

"What's so surprising about me being nice?" she wanted to know. "I'm nice all the time. You just aren't paying attention."

I started to point out that Mae did pay attention, and so did I. In fact, I'd even noticed that she seemed a little competitive with the Golden Lion and the Parisian Light earlier. But what was the purpose of arguing? We needed to figure out our next steps.

"I almost forgot!" Akiko went on. "The Golden Lion slipped me this note. She said they couldn't figure it out. What do you think it says?"

Unfolding the paper, she held it out for the three of us to see.

G S A E S C E
U T V S E R T

Twenty-Five

*W*E STARED AT THE NOTE AS AKIKO smoothed it out on her knees. The penciled letters were neat and clear. I squinted at them, imagining the words I could form if I scrambled them up. I heard Akiko and Mae doing the same.

"'Gas,' 'sag,' 'sage,'" Mae suggested.

"I think I see a bad word in the top line," said Akiko. "And on the bottom line, there's 'use,' 'vest,' 'rest.'"

I shook my head. This secret message seemed different. I didn't think it was a word scramble. There was something more here.

"Should we hold it up to a mirror?" I asked. "Or check for invisible ink?"

The walls shook again. Akiko, Mae, and I scooted closer together on our stretch of the train tracks. I noticed one of the little ones next to us began to cry, while the moms and the other siblings tried to cheer him up. My heart squeezed in my chest imagining Baby Lou crying. I hoped Vinnie was there to make him feel safe. I'd be home with them again soon, and when I was, I'd make sure to read them all the comic books they wanted. Especially ones with Nova the Sunchaser, Hopscotch, and Hauntima.

Time passed as we finished Akiko's chocolate bar and kept on trying to crack the message. Was it an hour? Longer?

Finally Mae perked up. She grabbed the note and stared closely at it, her nose nearly touching the paper. Akiko had nodded off on my shoulder, so when I jumped to attention, she did too.

"What is it?" Akiko asked groggily. "Can we leave now?"

"I think I've got it," whispered Mae excitedly. "Have you got a pencil and paper, Akiko?"

We knew she did. And once they were produced, we watched Mae's pencil scratch across the page. She wrote out each letter, just as it was on the original paper. Then she began drawing lines from letters in the top row to the ones below, connecting them in a long zigzag.

"It looks like you're drawing a backyard fence, Mae," I

whispered, watching her link one letter to the next, up and down.

"That's exactly what you call this kind of cipher!" she exclaimed as quietly as she could. "It's a rail-fence cipher! Or at least I think that's what this is. Look!"

G S A E S C E
U T V S E R T

"G-U-S. 'Gus'?" began Akiko, trying to make sense of it. "G-U-S-T. 'Gust'? 'Gusta'?"

I had never seen a rail-fence cipher before. But I liked it already. Akiko passed me a pencil and paper, and I began writing the same two lines on my own page. I made sure to offset the letters a little bit, the way they were in the note. Then I traced the letters up and down, just as Mae had shown us.

And there it was: a word I didn't know, followed by a word I did.

"G-U-S-T-A-V-E-S," I whispered. "I have no idea what that means. But the second part! It looks like S-E-C-R-E-T."

"That spells 'secret,'" said Akiko, still working it out. I could hear her breathing as she concentrated. "Hauntima's ghost! What in the world does 'gustaves' mean? And why are they secret?"

We stared into one another's faces. None of us spoke. The soft murmurs of the nearby kids echoed off the tunnel's tiled walls. The air down here was chilly despite the summer warmth outside. The smell was terrible.

"We've got to figure out the meaning of 'gustaves,'" said Mae, rearranging her legs and trying to get comfortable. "Is it a place? A person? An object? Or maybe something you do, like 'She *gustaves* flowers'?"

"But we can't just think about this message, Mae," said Akiko, picking at the chocolate crumbs left on the wrapper. "We've got to figure out what we're going to do now—"

"Now that we're not superheroes," I said. "Akiko is right. We still need to save Zenobia. We've got to find a way to get over to France, to reach the Eiffel Tower."

Mae went quiet and stared at her lap.

"Don't forget Aunt Willa and Aunt Janet," she reminded us. "The Metallic Falcon has them both in his horrible clutches. They need us too."

Akiko and I nodded. Mae must have felt sick with worry about her aunts. My stomach was always knotted up like a pretzel about Mam, Cousin Kay, and my little brothers. My dad, too, or at least the memory of him.

Akiko let out a deep sigh.

"Look around this place," she whispered. "London is one of the greatest cities on earth. And its people are hiding out underground, sleeping in the subway to escape attacks from this enemy. We've got to do whatever we can to help."

We heard the faint bark of a dog. It was quickly hushed, and I realized it was probably not supposed to be down here. Someone must have sneaked it in. Probably because it was too fragile to be left behind. Or too loved.

"Astra," I whispered, knowing that we'd have smuggled him down here with us. "And Mrs. B." I paused, trying to push away the worry. "I really wish we could reach them. But without our powers, we've probably lost touch with Room Twelve."

"Oh no!" whispered Mae, her expression tight. "That means we can't let them know about the message—'gustaves secret.' We can't ask them what it means."

And the realization seemed to hit all three of us at the same time.

We were on our own in this fight after all.

"I know I didn't seem very positive earlier," Akiko said softly. "Sometimes I doubt myself. When we're in our capes, masks, and boots, I feel every bit a superhero. But when it's just plain old me—Akiko Nakano, kid with asthma and allergic to practically everything under the sun—well, then it's hard for me to remember anything I'm good at."

I held my breath.

This was exactly how I felt too.

"But then I have to remind myself that we do have things we're good at," Akiko said. "We each have things that make us pretty special. So we're going to have to use them now."

She was right. No matter what was ahead, we were going to have to stand up and fight with whatever we had.

"Mrs. B would ask one thing of us," I said. "To try."

Mae looked up into my face, then into Akiko's. "I think that's what bravery is, when it comes down to it. Knowing the things that scare us—all the things that could go wrong, the ways we could fail—and pushing through anyway.

"Bravery," she said, letting out a sigh, "means trying."

Twenty-Six

*I*T WAS THE MIDDLE OF THE NIGHT WHEN Mae woke Akiko and me. She pressed her finger to her lips and pointed toward the ceiling, gesturing for us to quietly leave the underground shelter and return to London's streets.

It took me only seconds to shake the cobwebs from my mind and snap back to the moment. Sleeping shapes were lying all around us, some of them snoring, most of them snuggled in close beside family members. The children next to us were piled on top of each other like puppies, using one another's body heat to keep warm. I silently wished them well, then turned to follow Mae up the escalator, picking my way past even more people as they slept.

Once we reached the street, the smell of smoke hung thick like a wall. Crews were working up and down the neighborhood, putting out fires both large and small. The only light came from the flames. Like American cities, London was under a nighttime blackout. So there were no streetlamps lighting our way, and the moon was nowhere to be found. I couldn't even see a single star.

We made our way through the city, eventually finding a road that led to an airfield just on the edge of town. As we followed a path that skirted the grounds, we stared at the aircraft parked inside hangars and hidden under tarps.

"It wouldn't exactly be stealing," I whispered as we stared at the smallest airplane on the tarmac. "We'd return it."

"Right," agreed Akiko. "We would simply be borrowing it. We have every intention of giving it back."

Mae nodded her head confidently, as if trying to convince herself.

But then she seemed to come to her senses.

"Wait, steal a plane?" she said, her voice going a little higher. "A plane you want to fly? I mean, you want *me* to fly? I am not good enough to get us to Paris! It's one thing to mess around on training equipment with my aunts. It's another thing entirely to try to fly one of those things across the English Channel!"

I ducked lower into the bushes and pulled Mae and Akiko down with me. Even though it was dark, I didn't want to risk getting caught. And it looked as if Mae had already forgotten about our pep talk—the one about each of us having talents to share.

"Nobody seems to be in the office right now," Akiko said, pointing at a shack near the runway. "I bet we can get the maps we need and even use their radio. Let's go!"

And she took off across the tarmac. I watched her slip into the shadows by the wooden shed. I crept along quickly behind her. Thankfully, I could hear Mae's footsteps following mine.

Once inside the shed, I ran straight to one of the desks where maps were spread out. With Mae's help, we began plotting out a route. I tried to remember the math equations Cousin Kay had taught me, accounting for the wind and the weather we would be facing tonight. As I did some of the calculations, Mae chewed nervously on a pencil. I decided to roll up two of the maps and bring them with us, along with a compass and a watch that were sitting nearby. We'd borrow them all for a bit, I told myself, then return them later with the plane.

When I looked across the room, I saw Akiko seated at a radio, headset over her ears, and tapping out a Morse code message. It reminded me of Noor Khan, the spy we'd met in San Francisco. She had planned to parachute into

France to help the Resistance. I wondered if Noor was out there somewhere tonight.

"There's a message coming back to us!" said Akiko, jumping to her feet. "It says . . ." She sat back down at the table. We waited as her pencil scratched across the page.

"It says 'You're not alone! Don't give up! From your friend the Light.'"

"Do you think that came from the Parisian Light?" I asked, wondering if we could reach Room Twelve after all.

"Or maybe it's from Noor Khan," said Mae. "In Arabic, *Noor* means 'light.'"

Whoever sent it, that message was exactly what the three of us needed to hear just then.

"What message did you send?" asked Mae, tugging on an aviator's helmet.

"I'm hoping Zenobia hears it. I said help is on the way," Akiko said breathlessly. "And I didn't even bother to make it secret. There's no time for that. We've got to go now, while it's dark and nobody sees us."

Akiko and I grabbed leather helmets, and Mae found goggles for each of us. Then we pulled on the smallest leather jackets we could find. But before we reached the door, a light turned on across the way.

Somebody was awake.

We were caught.

"Three kids climbing into a plane? That is going to

draw suspicion!" Mae announced. I thought she was ready to run away. But instead, she seemed suddenly eager to reach the plane as fast as she could. "Akiko, climb onto my shoulders. And, Josie, grab that trench coat. The three of us are going to become one pilot."

"Just like Mrs. B always says," Akiko said with a laugh. "When the three of us work together as one, we can do amazing things."

I helped Akiko hook a leg over one of Mae's shoulders, then the other. Then I grabbed a tan raincoat off a hanger and draped it over her shoulders. Akiko adjusted the leather helmet over her hair, then fixed the goggles at her eyes.

"What about me?" I asked, feeling panic bubbling up in my chest. "What should I do? I can see a mechanic over there. He's got a light on underneath one of the wings. What if he notices me?"

Mae opened the coat, letting me slip in beside her. Then Akiko tied the belt to keep it from flapping open. Pushing through the door, we shuffled outside and headed over to the smallest plane—the silver training plane we'd seen from the field—parked on the tarmac. Mae said it was an AT-6, known as "the Texan." She'd practiced in one of these with Aunt Willa.

"The mechanic," Akiko whispered, her voice sharp. "He's standing up now. He's spotted us! He's coming this way!"

"Act natural," hissed Mae, trying to keep Akiko balanced on her shoulders as we weaved past the parked aircraft. "Don't make him suspicious."

"Too late," Akiko croaked. "He started running! Let's get out of here!"

Mae and I staggered toward the small silver plane as fast as we could. When we reached the wing, we tumbled onto the tarmac. Akiko landed on the two of us, unharmed. Shedding the overcoat, Mae scrambled to her feet and jumped into the Texan's front seat. Akiko and I squeezed into the back.

"Hey, you kids!" came the mechanic's shouts. "What do you think you're doing?"

"Hurry, Mae!" I said, clutching Akiko's arm beside me. "He's getting closer!"

After a moment's hesitation, Mae began flipping switches and touching the instrument panel's dials and gauges. I heard her whispering to herself as she checked each one. Then, finally, she brought the engine roaring to life.

"Go, go, go!" Akiko shouted. "He's right behind us!"

"He's grabbing for the tail!" I called, barely able to control my panic. "Now, Mae!"

Suddenly we shot forward, hurtling across the grounds toward what I hoped was a runway. I thought my heart might burst out of my ribs like some sort of caged bird. The mechanic was running after our plane now, still shouting for us to stop.

Once she slid the canopy window closed, Mae pushed the Texan harder. I could feel the wheels rhythmically thumping as we sped faster and faster down the runway. Up ahead of us in the darkness, I could make out a silhouette of trees standing just beyond the airport. Were we going to run into them?

Thankfully, I felt us lift off the ground. But in the next moment, we bounced back to earth with a teeth-rattling jolt.

I was about to lose hope when, with another bounce or two, our wheels left the runway for good.

"We're flying!" Akiko called, exhaling the words in a heavy sigh of relief. I could feel us climbing into the blue-black sky. "We are actually flying!"

"You did it, Mae," I shouted, reaching my hand to thump her shoulder in the front seat. "You're just like Aunt Janet and Aunt Willa!"

Twenty-Seven

$\mathscr{P}$EERING THROUGH THE BUBBLE CANOPY over our heads, I watched the ground fall away beneath our wings. Barns and houses and streets looked like dark squares and rectangles below us in the night sky. The air grew as cold as December, and I was grateful for the warmth of my leather jacket as we climbed higher into cold, damp clouds.

"Without a cape!" Akiko called. "I can't believe we're flying to France without capes!"

"Not yet," Mae hollered back, evening out our wings from the initial teeter-tottering. "It's going to be a while before we reach Paris!"

There were so many ways that flying in a plane was different from flying with a cape. But the similarities were what I loved best: The cold air was just as invigorating, the view was just as stunning, and the stomach-flipping thrill was just as incredible.

I unrolled the maps and studied our route. We could fly due south until we reached the coast, near a town called Brighton. Then cross over the English Channel to France. I hollered up to Mae, listing a few landmarks to watch for.

"Look, Mae!" shouted Akiko. "Water ahead! Is that the English Channel?"

I gazed down at the water below us. The world looked peaceful, even calm. I noticed that the docks far below us appeared still. But I knew they'd be busy soon enough. And while the German bombers we'd encountered before seemed to have returned to their bases, we couldn't assume we were the only ones in the sky.

"It might be a little bumpy as we cross the Channel to France," Mae called over her shoulder. "Just hang on!"

"Josie and I will watch out for any danger," Akiko hollered. "From passing planes or thunderstorms or Nazi baddies."

At the thought of bad guys like the Metallic Falcon, a chill shivered through my bones. How would we battle him? Without superpowers? What if he got to Paris and Zenobia before us?

What could three ordinary kids possibly do in the face of such evil?

Time passed, and the clouds slowly melted away. The stars that twinkled now were the brightest I'd ever seen. I wanted to reach out and touch them. I wished I could identify more than just the Big Dipper. I bet Akiko knew at least some of the constellations. Mae too. But I didn't feel like asking. The three of us were mostly silent, alone with our thoughts as we made our way through the sky.

Akiko was the first to speak again, letting out a quiet cheer as she pointed at the land that suddenly came into view far below us. "That must be France. Noor is some-where down there." She pressed her forehead to the glass and stared at the dark landscape.

"My daddy too," said Mae, glancing to her right. "He's somewhere in France, driving his ambulance, helping get soldiers to safety."

We were quiet as the Texan droned steadily into the night. When Mae spoke again, Akiko and I leaned forward in our seats to catch her words.

"It's easy for me to imagine my daddy down there, doing whatever he can," she said, nodding slightly as if to reassure herself. "He's always had a kind heart. Even when I was little, maybe as far back as I can remember, he's been saving things. Stray dogs, lost cats, baby bun-nies, even caterpillars on the sidewalk. I guess that's why

I love animals so much—it's because of him."

She paused and looked over the plane's edge, as if she could see him down there below us.

"Once when I was turning five years old, there was a tornado," Mae went on. "It was the night of my birthday, and Granny Crumpler had baked me a cake. When she set it down before me, I took one look at the pretty, pale-blue icing, and I began to cry.

"I reminded Daddy about a bird's nest in the front yard, and the blue robin's eggs that were inside it. How would those helpless baby birds ever survive a tornado?"

Akiko called up to Mae asking what her daddy did. "He didn't go outside when a tornado was coming, did he?"

"He did," Mae said, nodding again. "We heard the roaring wind and the sound of trees snapping, so Granny said we'd eat our cake later. But as we headed for the basement to take shelter, Daddy raced out into the yard. When I ran to the window to make sure he was all right, I saw the tree break in half. I screamed, and Granny pulled me to the basement. I thought my father was gone forever."

I leaned closer toward her seat. "Was he hurt? Did the tree hit him?"

"Next thing I knew, Daddy was beside me on the sofa in the basement, cupping the nest safely in his hands and asking me to count the five blue robin's eggs—five gifts for my fifth birthday, he said."

Akiko and I smiled. These were the types of memories I held on to so tightly, to keep my dad close. And I knew Akiko must do the same for her family.

"Did you name them?" Akiko asked. "All the robin's eggs—did you give each one a name?"

"You bet we did." Mae laughed. "Ralphie, Rocky, Ricky, Rosie, and Rapunzel. Daddy was always giving animals names. Now you know where I got it."

We flew on, letting Mae's story warm us like a favorite blanket. After a while, I noticed faint lights off my side of the plane. They were dotting the countryside below us. I nudged Akiko, and she leaned over to study them too.

"I think those lights are for small planes like ours," she said, pushing her goggles up. "Noor Khan talked about them. They are flashlights. Resistance fighters sneak into fields and light the way for small planes to land."

Mae could hear us. "It's incredibly dangerous. I learned about this when we were in San Francisco. The planes fly in from England, like we're doing. Pilots like me follow those flashlights and land right there in the farm fields. They bring in whatever supplies the Resistance fighters need to fight the Nazis—money, weapons, clothing."

I stared down at the faint lights so far below us. I imagined who was in the field and holding up the flashlights. Resistance fighters. They could be men or women, grandparents, schoolteachers, mechanics, dog lovers. They might even be kids like us.

It reminded me of Mrs. B's words. We're not alone in this fight.

Soon the pasture and the pale signals disappeared, and we flew deeper into the blue night. Akiko and I slumped against each other and scanned the sky for any trouble. The engine droned on and on, but it didn't lull us to sleep. We were much too charged to possibly nod off. My mind raced with worries about what we might find once we reached Paris. And while Akiko and Mae were both quiet too, I knew their minds were probably churning with the same thoughts.

A few times, I heard the faint droning of a plane's engine in the distance. But nothing came too close to our path. And from what I could tell in the blue light around us, there were no thunderstorms on the horizon.

I was just turning to Akiko to ask about the weather, when the hair rose on the back of my neck. Something had moved in the sky beside us. Like a sixth sense, a feeling swept over me.

We had company.

"Akiko!" I said. "Did you see that? Over there—off to the right?"

She whipped her head up, eyes searching the sky. After a moment or two, she shrugged. Nothing.

"Maybe I'm just seeing things," I said, adjusting my aviator's goggles.

But there it was again, this time to the left, off Akiko's side. Was it a spark from our engine? A swarm of fireflies? A shooting star? I bumped her shoulder, pointing. Again we watched out for anything unusual.

"Hey, what is that?" Akiko said, pressing her hand to the glass. "I saw it, Josie. No, I *felt* it. Something's out there!"

I still couldn't see a plane or a parachute nearby. But I definitely had a feeling that something was in the sky keeping pace beside us, coming in closer and swooping underneath our plane. It seemed to change sides every few minutes, on our right, then appearing moments later on our left.

"Josie? Akiko?" came Mae's worried voice from the front seat. "I've got a feeling."

I waited for Mae to go on, but she didn't. Instead, I saw her scanning the sky ahead of us like a searchlight, wary of danger. All three of us were on high alert. Was the Metallic Falcon about to swoop down? Was a Nazi plane tailing us?

Suddenly another flash of light caught my eye, this time in the sky just above our canopy window.

"There it is again!" I shouted, jabbing my finger in the air. "Mae! Watch out!"

Twenty - Eight

"FINALLY, I'VE TRACKED YOU DOWN."

Mae startled, and the plane did a little hiccup. "Who said that?" she squeaked from the front seat. "Akiko, are you messing around?"

"That wasn't me!" Akiko protested, her voice just as high pitched. "Josie?"

"Not me, either!" I answered. "But I know who it's got to be! Nova!"

Pop!

A moment later, just off the tip of our right wing, Nova the Sunchaser's glider appeared. The sun wasn't up yet, but the sky was starting to fill with hints of color. Puffy clouds of salmon pink were beginning to bloom low on the eastern horizon, blending to a rich blue above us. I'd never seen anything so beautiful in my life.

"Nova," cheered Akiko, "thank goodness!"

"What a relief," agreed Mae, glancing to the wing.

In the pale light, I had to squint to see the sleek lines and sharp angles of Nova's plane. It reminded me of the paper airplane we'd folded back in Chicago. Her ponytail whipping in the wind, I couldn't help but gape in grateful amazement at the ghostly sight of her.

Judging by the angry expression on her face, however, Nova the Sunchaser wasn't especially overjoyed at the sight of us. Using superpowers, she made sure we all heard her.

"What in the world do you think you're doing?" she shouted. "Do you know how dangerous this is? At any moment you could be attacked! And not just by the Metallic Falcon, but by Germ—"

"We know the dangers!" said Akiko, not quite whining. "But, Nova, we can't let Zenobia down! She needs us!"

"All the superheroes need us," I added, shouting to be heard.

"And my aunts," reminded Mae. "We've got to bring them back too!"

Nova shook her head angrily. "Room Twelve never abandons its operatives!"

Something caught in my mind hearing that. Was Nova talking about Mae's aunts? That they were somehow part of

Room Twelve too? But that was impossible. Wasn't it?

Before I could ask, Nova rolled her glider up and over us, settling into place on our left side now. Mae kept the wings steady as we flew side by side into the brightening sky.

"I understand," Nova called over. "I really do. Hauntima's ghost, the three of you have done so much already! But this . . . what's ahead . . . we cannot let you!"

Mae, Akiko, and I protested. We'd already come so far. I thought of Aunt Willa and Aunt Janet. I thought of Zenobia and her messages, each one more desperate than the last. I thought of all the superheroes who, like us, had lost their powers. And peering below us, I thought of what we'd seen in the darkness: the flashlights lighting the way into pastures for planes to land.

There were so many people battling evil as best they could.

We were on this plane because we were part of the same fight.

"It's too late," called Akiko, her voice gravelly as she shouted. "There's no way we can turn back now."

Nova shook her head. She said something about Room Twelve and danger and going too far.

"Akiko's right," hollered Mae, a little frantically. "There really is no turning back!"

And suddenly she dipped our plane to the right and swooped lower, causing my stomach to drop like I'd jumped off the high dive at the swimming pool.

"We've been spotted!" she hollered as Akiko and I screamed. "Hang on!"

Two planes zoomed across our path, causing all three of us to duck. My chest rattled from the vibrations of their engines. Mae let out a long breath of air and clutched the stick to steady our plane.

"Hauntima's ghost!" Akiko croaked. "That was much too close!"

We spun around in our seat and watched the fliers zoom away. I recognized the black mark on their tails. They were German planes.

The landscape below us was full of buildings and streets now. Gone were the green pastures of the farmlands. We must have reached the city limits of Paris. I figured that meant we were closer to finding Zenobia. But closer to the Nazi military too.

All at once the *rat-a-tat* of bullets sliced the air. We couldn't let ourselves get distracted! I looked all around for the Eiffel Tower. Surely a structure as tall as that could be seen from miles away.

"There it is," hollered Akiko. She was pointing ahead of us and showing Mae. "Do you see it, just off to the right?"

Flashes behind us caught my eye, and I saw the wings of the two German planes light up, as if they were under attack. But I couldn't see who was doing the attacking.

It was as if it were coming out of thin air. Akiko turned around with me, and we focused on the scene behind us.

"Nova!" shouted Akiko, the realization suddenly dawning on her. "She must have gone after those planes!"

"You're right," I said, hollering into Akiko's ear. Then I called up to Mae, "Did you hear that? Nova's protecting us!"

Mae peeked down at the city below us, then let out a queasy groan.

"Oh boy," she said. "The street is really, really far down."

"No, Mae, don't start on the scared-of-heights thing," Akiko said. "You're past that! Look how great you've done!"

I squeezed Mae's shoulder, trying to urge her on. She wasn't really scared of heights. She'd told us before: She was scared of making a mistake. Looking over the edge right now reminded her of what was at stake. It reminded her of letting down Aunt Willa and Aunt Janet and everyone she loved.

"Don't think about all the ways things could go wrong, Mae," I called up to her. "Look at all the things you've done right! You've already been incredibly brave—just like your dad!"

"Thanks for the encouragement," Mae yelled over her shoulder. But this time, her voice sounded shaky. "Because Josie, Akiko—we're really going to need to be brave. Look!"

Twenty-Nine

I STRAINED TO SEE THROUGH THE CANOPY up ahead, hoping to catch sight of the thing that had Mae so worried.

"What do you mean?" I asked. Akiko craned her neck beside me.

But before Mae could answer, a low hum reached my ears. Suddenly everything came into focus. And what I saw sent a small earthquake through my whole body.

German planes—even more than we'd seen over London. They were swarming the sky ahead of us, and their terrifying shapes hung in the air like deadly hornets. How could

Nova the Sunchaser possibly keep them all away? When she was just a ghost of her former self? It would be too much for her to take on alone!

"They're everywhere," whispered Akiko, her eyes as big as plums beneath her goggles. "How in the world will we get past them?"

I had the same question.

There was no way our Texan could escape now, as they seemed to already have us circled. If we tried to flee, they'd be on us in a flash.

"I see the Eiffel Tower," Mae called back to us. "What should I do?"

In the distance, behind the deadly German swarm, I spotted the graceful black spire of the Eiffel Tower rising into the sky. Zenobia and the others were there—so close! But what if we couldn't reach them in time?

A spark of light off to the left of our plane drew my attention. It was Nova again, soaring faintly beside us.

"We've got it this time, Nova," I called to her. "Don't risk everything for us!"

I wasn't exactly sure we really could do it on our own. But I couldn't bear the thought of Nova getting hurt. We weren't the Infinity Trinity anymore, and that single thought made my blood run as cold as a milkshake. And from the sound of Akiko's frantic breathing, she was feeling it too.

Powerless.

The word bounced around my head like a Ping-Pong ball. When we were in San Francisco, Zenobia had messaged to let us know that she and the other superheroes had no powers. Nova, Hopscotch, and Hauntima had done all they could to mentor us, but their powers were being drained—right before our eyes. And Mrs. B and Astra had shown us the way, but they were too weakened to fight beside us now.

It really was up to Mae, Akiko, and me—but without our capes, masks, and boots. This wasn't exactly the way the league of secret heroes had planned. But we still had to push on.

I shook out my hands, trying to keep them from trembling at the thought of the Metallic Falcon. He'd nearly vaporized us, leaving us as powerless as the rest of the superheroes. How in the world were we going to get past swarms of Nazi fighters and defeat a supervillain as powerful as that sinister metal bird?

"I don't know how we'll do it, but we can't let them down," I said, leaning forward in my seat so Mae could hear me. "Too many people are depending on us!"

Images of my little brothers, Mam, and Cousin Kay flooded my mind. Akiko squeezed her eyes shut, and I knew she was thinking of Tommy. Not to mention her mom and the rest of her family.

And Mae—how was she handling all of this pressure? Her daddy was driving an ambulance on a battlefield somewhere below us, and her beloved aunts were in the clutches of the dreaded Metallic Falcon. Granny Crumpler was probably frantic, too, wondering where we'd gone.

"Look out, Mae!" called Akiko suddenly. "Another plane's coming toward us—from over there!"

She was pointing over my shoulder, where a familiar blue-colored aircraft was roaring straight in our direction. Its nose was painted to look like a shark, with jagged white teeth and a ferocious snarl. The effect was terrifying!

"Shark! How can we shake it?" I shouted. "It's getting closer, Mae!"

"That's a Messerschmitt," said Mae. "A German fighter plane!"

Despite the engine roaring in our ears, we could hear the menacing drone of the shark-plane getting closer. At the last moment, it dipped just below us. Through its canopy window, I could see the German pilot, his brown goggles similar to the ones we were wearing.

Then panic seized my chest, and I grabbed for Akiko's arm.

"Look inside," I said, almost unable to push the words from my mouth. "He's not alone in there!"

"Hauntima's ghost," wheezed Akiko, following the plane with her eyes. "You're right, Josie. That's Aunt Willa!

And Aunt Janet too! Mae's aunts are in that shark-plane!"

We hollered at Mae to trail the German fighter, all three of us frantic not to let it out of our sight. Dangerous-looking bombers and sleek attack planes circled the sky like a deadly swarm. I could feel their menacing hum in my chest. It made my heart race even faster.

The two figures we'd seen on board the Nazi plane were definitely Mae's aunts. But now that we knew where they were, what were we supposed to do? Chase them down until we landed somewhere on the Paris streets below? I'd heard radio announcers talk about dogfights, but we were in no position to engage a German plane in battle. What was our next move?

Suddenly a shadow passed before the sun.

"The Metallic Falcon!" Akiko shouted over the dull roar of our engine. Ducking lower in our seats, we stared up at the terrifying sight of his wide metal wings outstretched above us. "We've got to get out of here!"

His voice thundered. And the booming flash that followed made me realize how dangerous his rage would be.

"Where are those little gnats?" he shouted. "Doesn't the Infinity Trinity care about rescuing the lady pilots? I thought snatching those fliers would guarantee a showdown with those brazen brats! Why haven't they fallen into our trap?"

He thrashed angrily through the sky, lashing out at anyone who was near him. And seconds later, I saw two planes and their pilots transformed into iron statues. Not far from us, they fell from the sky like rocks. My heart clutched in my chest as I thought of Aunt Willa and Aunt Janet.

"Did you hear him?" shouted Mae over her shoulder. "The message we caught, saying the TRAP IS SET! The Metallic Falcon was talking about us! He kidnapped my aunts as a *trap*! To fight us!"

"Don't let him catch us, Mae!" I yelled to her. "That metal maniac wants nothing more than to destroy us!"

I braced myself as Mae rolled our plane to the right, still following the shark-plane.

"Not exactly," called Akiko. "Did you listen to what that bird-brain said? He's looking for the Infinity Trinity!"

"We know, Akiko," I said. "We've got ears!"

Akiko shook her head in exasperation, as if I weren't catching on.

"Josie, don't you see? He's on the lookout for super-heroes! For green capes, orange masks, and purple boots! He's not expecting three kids to show up instead!"

My jaw dropped open like a broken drawer. Akiko was right! The Metallic Falcon was ready for battle, but not with three ordinary kids. He was searching the sky for superheroes.

Maybe losing our superpowers wasn't so bad.

Maybe it was the only way we could ever slip past a supervillain like him!

*T*HAT'S IT, RIGHT?" SHOUTED MAE. "THE SHARK-plane, up ahead and to the left. It's the one?"

I knew it was. None of us had taken our eyes off that eerie aircraft since we'd spotted Aunt Willa and Aunt Janet inside.

"Keep after him, Mae," I told her. "The Metallic Falcon has his eyes out for the Infinity Trinity. He won't give this plane a second thought."

"That's fine," said Akiko. "But how do we rescue your aunts, Mae? It's not as if we can just shoot down the shark-plane."

I wondered what to do. Her aunts couldn't parachute out of the German bomber. That could turn ugly with so many Nazi planes buzzing the skies. And there was no way to radio them and let them know we were here to help.

"I don't know," I said, wishing I could come up with a good idea. "If only we could get close enough so your aunts could jump into our plane. But that's impossible."

"And Nova," said Akiko sadly, her eyes searching the sky. "Who knows where she is now? Between the Metallic Falcon and the German planes, she might have . . ." And she trailed off, unable to finish. The thought of losing Nova the Sunchaser was too much for any of us to think about.

Mae was silent as we trailed behind the German bomber. It swung wide in its arc over the city. But it maintained a steady orbit, with the Metallic Falcon at its center.

"There is one thing." Mae's voice was tight, and I knew she must have been a nervous wreck. "Aunt Willa's warned me over and over about this one particular trick. It can happen to pilots when they're doing loops and acrobatics."

"So," croaked Akiko, "what does that have to do with the shark-plane?"

Mae inhaled deeply, then let the air out in a slow, steady breath. I could hear her speaking, but I had to lean closer to understand her. At first her words were too low. But a moment later, they took shape in my ears. She was talking to herself.

"Be brave. Be brave. Be brave."

This was Mae's moment. All her worries about flying, about making a mistake, about letting everybody down—it was all right here in this moment. I looked at Akiko, unsure what to do. Slowly she reached her hand up and rested it on Mae's arm. I did the same. Without a word, we let her know we understood. And we believed in her.

"Hang on!" she shouted. And my stomach dropped again as Mae rolled our plane. Now we seemed to be heading in the opposite direction as the shark-plane carrying her aunts. Akiko and I whipped around to stare behind us, afraid we'd lose them.

"What are you doing, Mae?" I shouted. "They're flying the other way!"

But Mae shook her head, telling us to keep our eyes on the shark. She pushed our Texan faster through the sky, holding steady at an altitude just below the other German aircraft.

"We're going to force the shark pilot into a climb—a steep one!" she called over her shoulder. "I'm betting that if I can surprise him, my aunts will know just what to do!"

Akiko grabbed binoculars from her Hauntima bag and trained them on the shark-plane. Her cheeks were turning a familiar pink, and while it was too noisy to hear her breathing, I knew Akiko was as nervous as I was. My heart seemed to have flown to my throat, beating fast like a hummingbird's wings.

"What if we lose them?" Akiko shouted to Mae. "Should you get behind them again?"

"Mae, where are you taking us?" I added, leaning closer to her ear in the seat ahead. "We can't run away!"

But Mae pushed the Texan even faster, leaning forward as if she were flying by cape instead of by engine. We sliced through the sky.

"We're not running away from this," Mae said calmly. "We're running toward it."

Before I could ask her what she meant, Akiko sat up higher in her seat and excitedly tucked her feet underneath her. Again she pressed the binoculars to her eyes, peering ahead of us now instead of behind.

"The shark-plane!" she said. "Mae, it's coming right at us—fast!"

And even without binoculars, I could see the snarling front of the German pilot's plane getting closer. I fidgeted with the seat belt that crossed my and Akiko's laps as Mae held the Texan steady, never flinching. We were on a direct path to collide.

"Mae!" I shrieked. "If you've got one of Aunt Willa's tricks, this might be the time to use it!"

"Now!" howled Akiko, grabbing hold of the back of Mae's seat. "Do something!"

And just as we braced for the collision, the shark-plane gave way, shooting straight up into the air like a bottle rocket on the Fourth of July. Mae must have done the same maneuver, because suddenly Akiko and I were flung backward in our seats. All I could see was blue sky as the nose of our Texan climbed up, up, up, as if we were shooting at the sun.

"Hold on, you two," Mae called to us. "We're throwing this Nazi for a loop!"

"What does that mean?" shouted Akiko.

Akiko and I clutched the edges of the cockpit and pressed our feet beneath Mae's chair. My head was pinned to the back of my seat as we soared higher and higher into the sky. I knew exactly what Mae meant: We were looping through the air like we were part of a circus show, curling through the sky the way Aunt Willa and Aunt Janet had done just days before, when we chased the spies.

I closed my eyes, picturing the shark-plane that carried Mae's aunts performing the same heart-stopping loop.

Mae pushed our plane even harder, and I had a strange dizzying sensation. My body began sagging under a heavy pressure. And as I looked out on the horizon, the color started to drain from the sky.

My thoughts felt thick and slow. Was I passing out?

"Tense all your muscles or you could lose consciousness," Mae shouted to us. "Force your blood to flow!"

Suddenly the ground was right in front of us, and

the sky was at our feet! I grabbed hold of the seat-belt strap and yelled for Akiko to do the same. The pull on my body felt tremendous, as if I were weighed down with lead.

But Akiko didn't seem to be as alarmed as I was.

"Roller coaster!" she shouted, and I could hear the smile on her face.

Once we were right side up again, I looked all around for the shark-plane. I spotted it, off to our left. Now we were chasing after the German fighter plane instead of barreling toward it! The plane's wings teetered unsteadily ahead of us.

Mae's leather helmet was lopsided now. I could hear her talking to herself again—"Steady now"—as she adjusted her goggles and caught her breath.

"It's falling!" I yelled. "Oh no! The shark-plane is going into a spiral, like water draining from a bathtub!"

But as quickly as it dropped toward the ground, the German plane suddenly righted itself. It was as if the pilot had come to his senses and took control of the steering equipment.

We watched the shark-plane climb back into the sky and steady out. Mae pushed the Texan to catch up, and in a few short minutes we were flying just above them. Keeping up with their pace, Mae, Akiko, and I peered over the edge to see what was happening inside. The shark-plane's canopy window was like a clear bubble, and we could see two figures looking up at us.

"They're waving," Akiko exclaimed. "It's Aunt Willa and Aunt Janet, and they're waving as if nothing's wrong!"

"And the pilot?" Mae asked.

I squinted, trying to make out the slumped figure of the man in the leather helmet and goggles we'd seen before. "It looks like he's passed out!"

Mae pumped her fists in the air, cheering and whooping as the shark-plane peeled off over the outskirts of the city. It soared away from us, in the opposite direction of the Metallic Falcon and the other Nazi planes.

"Mae," I hollered, "you did it!"

"He blacked out," she said, trying to explain. "At least, I think he did! The g-force got him. Sometimes when pilots push their planes really fast, the gravitational forces are too much. All their blood pools into their legs, not their brains. It can make them 'gray out'—meaning they don't see color anymore. Or they 'black out'—meaning they're completely zonked."

And when the pilot passed out, that left Aunt Willa and Aunt Janet to take over.

Akiko and I were stunned. How in the world had Mae pulled this off? Aunt Willa must have been an amazing teacher. I wondered how many extra shifts at Gerda's Diner I would have to work in order to pay for flying lessons once we were back home.

"I hope they can get someplace safe," Akiko said, turning backward in her seat and watching the shark-plane piloted by Mae's aunts fly farther into the distance. "Who knows what the Metallic Falcon will do next?"

KABOOM!

We got our answer.

Thirty-One

"COME OUT, COME OUT, PESKY PIXIES!"

His booming voice sent a sort of shock wave rippling through the sky. "It's time to meet your destiny, Caped Kiddies!"

In his rage, the Metallic Falcon swatted a nearby plane from the sky. It crashed into a tall building.

"Get us out of here, Mae!" I whispered, choking on my words.

"Now!" added Akiko.

Mae pointed the nose of our plane toward the Eiffel Tower. I was grateful to see a wide patch of open land stretching out not far from it. My stomach lurched as the Texan plummeted downward, but I didn't mind. We couldn't get away from that tantrum-throwing bird fast enough.

"I'm going to try to land over there, in that park," Mae called. "Hang on!"

The engine slowed as we dipped lower, just above the Paris rooftops. I could see trucks and cars on the streets below us and people walking on the sidewalks. Nazi banners hung from some of the buildings—the horrible red with the black symbol in the middle that reminded me of a squashed spider.

Mae steered toward the park, and we dropped lower over the city blocks. The wings of our plane dipped to one side, then the other, and I couldn't help but wish for Akiko's teleportation powers right about now. The faster we could get out of this plane, the better. But we were powerless, I reminded myself. Teleportation was for the Orange Inferno, not plain old Akiko.

"Breathe," I heard Mae telling herself. "Easy does it, nice and smooth."

As we approached the park, the Eiffel Tower grew bigger and bigger in front of us. It was enormous, even more spectacular than I'd imagined from photographs. And while I knew it was made of heavy iron, it rose gracefully into the sky as if weightless. Its soaring arches and crisscrossing spire seemed to touch the sun.

"Look out, Mae!" hollered Akiko. "That building!"

As I pulled my eyes away from the Eiffel Tower, I saw what Akiko was warning about. There was one last building ahead of us, and we were coming in too low. At the speed we were flying, we were going to clip the roof!

"Careful," I yelled, "we're too close!"

The plane's wings teetered again as Mae tried to steady us. I braced myself for the impact, certain that the tail of our plane was going to hit the edge of the building. It was so near, I could have reached out a hand and touched the chimney.

But suddenly we lifted into the air again, as if billowed on a cloud. The plane's wings evened out, and we flew on until we touched down in the center of the green field.

"We're good!" shouted Mae. "Look at us! Safe and on the ground!"

With a final bone-rattling bounce, Mae brought the shiny silver Texan to a stop.

I'd never been more relieved to hit grass and dirt in my entire life.

"Well done," came a voice. And seconds later, Nova the Sunchaser and her sleek glider appeared, parked beside us. She seemed just as impressed as we were at Mae's flying skills. But I couldn't help wondering whether Nova had been hovering nearby. And for how long? She could put up a force field around her own plane. Had she done it for ours?

There was no time for distractions now, though. As we jumped out of the Texan, shedding our leather jackets and goggles, I quickly tried to think through a plan. "We need to reach the Eiffel Tower before too many people spot us. Let's go!"

Mae, Akiko, and I had just turned toward the tower when another passenger climbed from Nova's plane. "Hop to it!" she shouted, and the three of us froze on the spot. That call could only mean one thing.

Hopscotch!

"And look who else is with them," gawped Akiko as another rider climbed out. "Hauntima's ghost—"

"You're exactly right," Nova said with a laugh. "It *is* Hauntima. When I realized you weren't turning back, I summoned them to join me. You didn't really think the three of us could let the three of you go it alone. Did you?"

Mae's hands were shaking as she tugged off her goggles. *"None of us is ever truly alone in the fight,"* she whispered, her voice so soft I could barely hear her.

That's what Mrs. B had told us. And now I believed it. Not only were Nova, Hopscotch, and Hauntima here to help us, but I could feel my cousin Kay's spirit with us too, pushing us to try harder, work smarter, pay closer attention. And touching the wing of our Texan, I thought of my dad. He had loved flying. I know he'd have been so proud of Mae, Akiko, and me.

There really were so many people who were in this fight with us.

"Zenobia," I said, my mouth as dry as a sock, "she's somewhere in the tower. The others too. We need to get there as fast as we can."

Akiko fumbled with her Hauntima bag and pulled out a note. "Wait, look at this. Here's her last message, only we don't know what it means," she said, showing them the paper. "It was written in code, which was easy to crack. But we don't understand 'gustaves secret.' Do you know what 'gustaves' are?"

Hopscotch squinted beneath her mask as she read the message. She shook her head and passed it to Nova and Hauntima. None of them had any idea.

KABOOM!

Another explosion echoed across the park, and we knew the Metallic Falcon was continuing his angry attack. Not only would we need to keep clear of him as we crossed the open grounds to the tower, but we couldn't let ourselves get caught by the German planes buzzing overhead either.

"That bird is trying to stir up a battle," Hopscotch said, her face upturned. "He wants to draw out the Infinity Trinity so he can destroy them—and finally finish off the entire league of secret heroes."

Her words ran through me like an icy wind.

"But we have a secret weapon now," said Nova, turning to Mae, Akiko, and me. "You."

Us? A secret weapon?

"Without superpowers?" said Akiko, coughing. "What good are we?"

"Plenty good," answered Nova. "While the Metallic Falcon circles the sky waiting to pounce on the Infinity Trinity, you three will help us reach Zenobia and the others."

I gazed again at the enormous landmark up ahead. The Eiffel Tower was an icon to the world for a reason: It was incredible. Four sturdy legs rose from the ground, creating four arches that reached as high as my apartment building on Captain Flexor Street. And from that wide base, the tower shot straight up like an arrow piercing the clouds.

"The last message you were able to solve from Zenobia indicated the tower," said Hopscotch, signaling for Akiko, Mae, and me to get moving. "We don't have time to figure out 'gustaves secret.' So let's go with what we know. We must act now!"

Mae drew up short, and Akiko and I knocked into her back.

"Wait. Let's think," she said, nervously eyeing the Metallic Falcon as he flew above us. "We can't just walk right up to the tower. The Nazis are guarding it!"

"Mae's right," I said. "It's not like tourists are allowed up there with a war on, are they?"

Nova gave us an encouraging smile and put her hands on our shoulders.

"I'm glad you're so cautious," she said. "Hauntima, Hopscotch, and I came up with a plan. And we think it's good enough to get you onto one of the staircases in the tower's legs."

"After that, it's up to you. I know you'll succeed," said Hauntima. Her form was still ghostly, but her eyes looked fierce. "Hauntima wills it."

"Hop to it," Hopscotch added softly. And I could hear the worry in her voice.

"Time to shine," whispered Nova.

The three superheroes, their figures flickering in and out of intensity, faced us, standing shoulder to shoulder. Hopscotch closed her eyes and swept her arms out as if she were conducting an orchestra. She was using her conjuring powers to create something solid out of thin air.

We watched, wondering what it would be.

"Tires?" asked Akiko as something appeared on the dirt path beside us. "A car?"

"It's bigger than a car," whispered Mae. We watched in astonishment as the thing took shape. "A truck? She's almost done."

"A wagon," I said, unable to hide my shock. And when

the bright red cross on its side became clear, we all recognized what it was. "Hopscotch! You made an ambulance, out of thin air. That's brilliant."

Next Hauntima began to transform. We watched her beautiful face morph into an angry skull. "We will defeat these villains once and for all."

And in the blink of an eye, she shape-shifted into a new form. Where Hauntima had just been, now stood an ambulance driver—male—in full hospital uniform and cap. "Everyone, get inside the wagon!" she said in a deep voice. "Let's go!"

Akiko, Mae, and I jumped into the back of the wagon as Hopscotch and Nova climbed into the front beside Hauntima. We'd barely shut the door when the ambulance took off, tires screeching.

The street was busy with soldiers and trucks. Nova rolled down the windows, and the now-familiar buzz of planes swarming the sky streamed in. I saw everyday people walking hurriedly down side streets. It was clear to everyone in this part of Paris that trouble was brewing with the Metallic Falcon.

I tried to swallow despite the nervous lump in my throat.

"We're not far now," said Nova, turning to us from the front seat. "Once we've stopped near the Eiffel Tower's base, I'll create a distraction. You three can slip out of the ambulance and make your way up the tower stairs. Let's hope it's not too late to find Zenobia and the others."

Mae was seated in the middle between Akiko and me. She reached over and gave my hand a squeeze. Then Akiko's too. I felt a surge of something pass between us. But it wasn't the powerful jolt that happened when we transformed. Instead, it was something different. Something reassuring, like a promise.

"This is it," she said in a tight whisper.

"The three of us," said Akiko.

My heart pounded so loud and so fast, I was sure they could hear it. I tried to speak, but my words felt stuck. "It—it's up to us."

We were going to find Zenobia, and we'd do it without our capes, masks, or boots. We'd do it with our brains, our wits, and our courage. And if, somehow, we could free the missing superheroes to return to the skies and fight the world's evildoers once again, then all of us—including our families—would be safe.

I took a deep breath, the way I'd seen Mae do it. She closed her eyes beside me, and I heard Akiko whispering to herself. Then, from the front seat, came a distinctive *Pop!*

Nova had turned herself invisible.

As our ambulance idled at a street corner, waiting to pull up to the enormous base of the tower, I noticed the passenger door open. It was a slow movement, only wide enough to allow something slim to slip out of the front seat.

Then the door closed again, with a nearly silent click.

Alone in the front passenger seat now, Hopscotch snapped her fingers, conjuring a fashionable lady's hat. She slipped it on her head and rolled its black netting over her eyes. Suddenly she looked like a woman in mourning instead of the green-and-yellow superhero we adored.

Hauntima, still appearing as our male ambulance driver, beeped the horn impatiently. A few German soldiers moved out of the way to let us through.

I pressed my hand to my heart, trying to slow it down inside my chest. My eyes settled on the Nazi flag hanging from the tall arch ahead of us. I felt my jaw clench. How had they seized Paris? And so much of Europe? How was evil winning?

Suddenly a noisy crash sounded on the road behind us. Shouts rang out, and the soldiers began running to see what the commotion was all about.

"That's Nova!" said Hauntima from the driver's seat. "She's got them distracted. Now it's your turn—go!"

We slipped out the ambulance door and took off running toward the staircase as Hauntima and Hopscotch drove away. No one seemed to notice us. They were too busy craning their necks, curious to catch a glimpse of the ruckus Nova had created.

"That way," whispered Akiko, gesturing to the right. "I see a staircase! Come on!"

Mae raced behind her, and I followed quickly after Mae.

"Not so loud," I hissed as we bounded up the metal steps. "We'll catch their attention if we're too noisy. We've got to take each one silently!"

Somehow we managed to quiet our shoes on the narrow staircase. And, one by one, we began climbing up the Eiffel Tower steps.

And we climbed.

And we climbed.

Thirty-Two

*A*ND WE CLIMBED.

"Are you okay, Akiko?" asked Mae, after what seemed like an eternity. "You're slowing down."

"I'm fine," puffed Akiko. "Keep," she said, pausing to catch her breath, "going."

So we did. We pushed on and on, climbing higher and higher up the turning metal staircase. Every now and then, I peeked through the iron framework and saw the city streets falling away.

Before long, we heard voices.

Akiko stopped. Mae and I pressed in close behind her.

Trying to catch our breath without giving ourselves away, we tiptoed up the final few steps in silence. As the staircase gave way to an open area, we knew we had to be close to finding Zenobia.

"Two guards," I whispered, "far side." And I pointed toward a table near a wide railing that must have over-looked the city. "Watch out for others."

"And for Zenobia. Where could she be?" wondered Mae in a sharp whisper. "Surely she and the other super-heroes are here somewhere." And she ducked low and began slinking down the length of the railing opposite the guards. Akiko and I followed. We seemed to be heading for an office or a café—it was a room of some sort with metal beams and dark wood walls. Were the superheroes inside?

We reached the doorway. Just as my fingers closed on the knob to turn it, the door flew open! Mae, Akiko, and I jumped backward and hid in a shadow. Slowly a soldier stepped out into the sunshine. He was holding an open book and humming quietly to himself. He inhaled the fresh air deeply into his lungs, then let out a long sigh. I felt certain he would spot us at any moment and blow a whistle, drawing other German guards to arrest us!

But this soldier must have really liked his book. Because he walked on, humming the same quiet tune and turning the page. He never even noticed us.

"It's unlocked." Mae inched forward and slowly opened the door. "Keep low."

We slinked low on the floor and entered the room. Tables were pushed into a corner with chairs stacked on top. It probably had been a café of some sort, back in better times. There was a small wooden counter in front of us, where coffees were likely brewed.

Off to the left was another wooden door, this one a little narrower. Surely that led to the room where Zenobia was! Along with the other superheroes!

Finally, we'd found it!

Akiko was the first to get there. She pressed an ear to the wood and listened. Then she shook her head. "Nothing," she whispered. "No sound inside." She turned the knob and inched it open.

The three of us leaned forward to peer inside.

Suddenly something jumped at us! Mae gasped, and Akiko made a strange hiccuping sound. I covered my head with my arms, trying to shield myself from attack.

"A broom?" heaved Mae, catching it in one hand as she opened the door wider. "And a broom closet?"

"They're not here," said Akiko, dusting off her skirt. "Wherever Zenobia was when she sent those messages, it is not here."

"Then let's keep moving," I whispered, shutting the closet door and heading back for the staircase. "There's a second level to this tower, right? Maybe we'll find something if we climb higher."

We slinked back to where we'd begun, slipping onto the staircase and again climbing up, up, up. We took each step as quietly as we could, making sure not to draw the attention of the German soldiers at the tables—or anywhere else around here.

Without realizing it, I'd started counting our steps.

Sixty-four.

Eighty-eight.

One hundred thirty-seven.

Two hundred ninety-two.

"Finally," I said, huffing and puffing and dropping to my knees as we reached the second platform. "Three hundred twenty-four."

"Three hundred twenty-six," corrected Mae, who barely seemed to have broken a sweat. "I was counting too."

"Nope," said Akiko, her voice wheezy and her cheeks a bright pink as she bent over to catch her breath. "You're both wrong. There were three hundred twenty-seven steps." And after claiming victory, she collapsed backward onto the staircase and flung her arms and legs out. She looked like a wilted starfish.

"Don't get too comfortable, Akiko," warned Mae quietly. "We've got to keep moving. There might be German soldiers up here."

"Are you sure, Mae?" I asked, peeking around the corner and hoping we were alone. "Why would anybody be up here on the second platform of the Eiffel Tower? When there's a war on?"

The buzzing of those sinister German planes was even louder up here. At this height, we could see the whole city of Paris spread out in all directions. It was breathtaking, and a little scary. The Metallic Falcon's menacing shape was still circling the sky too, searching for the Infinity Trinity. I shivered as we watched his deadly wings open wide, allowing him to glide on the currents like an ordinary bird.

But he was anything but ordinary.

"Thank goodness he doesn't know where we are," I whispered.

"Or *who* we are," added Mae.

"We've got to make sure nobody finds us up here," said Akiko, looking around nervously now as we tiptoed from one side of the platform to the other. "We're so close to finding them. I just know it!"

Suddenly a noise caught our attention. It was a scraping sound, like a chair being pushed away from a table. Was someone coming for us?

"They're here," Mae whispered, dropping low to the ground and hurrying to hide behind a cluster of small tables. "German soldiers again!"

"You don't think it could be Zenobia, do you?" I asked as quietly—and hopefully—as I could.

But as we inched forward to investigate, a shout rang out. I nearly jumped out of my cotton socks!

"Hey! Why are you sneaking around?"

The accent was British. And cheerful as a burst of sunshine. "You told us exactly where to meet you!"

"*Oui!* The Golden Lion is right," came another voice, this one French. And I knew without looking that it was the Parisian Light. "We've been waiting for you all day. What took you so long?"

Thirty-Three

AFTER ALL THAT CLIMBING, MY KNEES melted like ice cream, and I was pretty certain they could not hold me up anymore. I collapsed into the nearest chair. Akiko and Mae took the ones beside me.

"Thank goodness it's you," I said, still glancing around the wide platform to make sure no soldiers were here. "The tower is full of Nazis!"

"How did you get past the Metallic Falcon?" asked Akiko. "He's circling the sky along with all those planes. It's incredibly dangerous right now!"

The Parisian Light explained how they were able to

disappear and reappear, sneaking past the angry super-villain. "It's not invisibility like Nova the Sunchaser's powers or conjuring like Hopscotch's. You see, when I use my power for matter manipulation, it means I can change something that already exists from one form into another."

The Golden Lion smiled proudly. "It was quite clever. She transformed us from human form into pigeons! We flew right below the Metallic Falcon and the Nazi planes, all the way to the second level here. It's a brilliant way to get around!"

Uh-oh. Akiko was not going to let that pass.

"Well, I think teleportation is pretty—"

"The Metallic Falcon's superpowers are the strongest we've ever seen," Mae said, thankfully heading off any new back-and-forth superpower debates—only this time between Akiko and the Parisian Light. "He's the one we should be focused on. Not only can he shoot heat beams and blast his powers to transform things into metal, but he has super-sight. He can see far into the distance as well as up close, like a microscope. We have to be careful. He's not going to miss anything!"

The Golden Lion and the Parisian Light nodded, say-ing they understood. "But really," said the Lion, "he's only after one thing. And that's the Infinity Trinity. It's all he's shouting about."

We fell silent. The familiar drone of plane engines filled the air. Then, like fingernails scraping a chalkboard, the Metallic Falcon's birdlike shrieks reached us. "Give me those superbrats!"

Mae sat up straighter in her chair.

"While he's distracted looking for the Emerald Shield, the Orange Inferno, and the Violet Vortex," she said, squaring her shoulders, "let's get busy."

She was right. We'd come too far, and the stakes were too high, for us to rest. We were in this fight, and we'd push on even without our capes, masks, and boots. We needed to reach Zenobia and the other superheroes. And we needed to make sure Mae's aunts were safe.

"Maybe you can help us," I said, forcing my voice not to shake. "We solved the message you gave us from Zenobia. It was her last. But we don't know what it means. Would you take a look?"

Akiko pulled the message from her bag and unfolded it.

"I'm sure you don't have any better guess at what 'gustaves secret' means than we do," Akiko began. She spread the paper on the table. "But it doesn't hurt to ask, right?"

The Golden Lion and the Parisian Light leaned forward, their eyes focused on the note. No words passed between them. But when they looked at each other, I saw a glimmer of something in their eyes. They both knew immediately what the message meant.

"No guesses, right?" Akiko said, folding the note up and slipping it back into her Hauntima bag. "Oh well, that's what I figured—"

"No guesses," agreed the Parisian Light, "because we know the answer!"

"What?" exclaimed Akiko. She looked a little annoyed.

"That's wonderful," said Mae, giving Akiko's shoe a quick kick. This was not the time for Akiko to get competitive about trivia knowledge and always being right. "What does it mean?"

The Parisian Light cleared her throat and gave Akiko a sideways glance. "There can be only one meaning to this. Because, you see, Gustave is the reason we are here."

Akiko made a funny noise. Even though she gestured for the Light to go on, I could tell she was annoyed that she wasn't the one solving this puzzle. But I was happy to have any answers.

"This place, the Eiffel Tower, was built by Gustave Eiffel," the Parisian Light explained. "The name 'Gustave' in the note must refer to him. To here!"

"We already knew about the Eiffel Tower. What about the *secret* part?" challenged Akiko. "What kind of secret did Gustave keep? It could be a million things. Everyone has secrets—"

"But his finest secret is right here," interrupted the Golden Lion, pointing to the ceiling above us. With her calm voice and gentle manner, she reminded me of Mae. "It's at the top of the tower itself."

Mae and I jumped.

"The top of the tower?" I asked, trying not to shout. "What do you mean? What's up there?"

All of us were on our feet now.

"When he finished building this tower," the Parisian Light said, "Gustave Eiffel created something for himself at the very top: an apartment. Nearly one thousand feet above the city! No one was allowed there—only the occasional guest. It was his secret hideaway."

"A secret hideaway?" I whispered, smacking a hand to my forehead. "Gustave Eiffel built a secret apartment at the top of his tower? *Gustave's secret!* So that must be where we'll find Zenobia and the others!"

Akiko mumbled something about how she probably would have figured it out on her own, eventually. I gave her shoe another poke.

"Where is the next staircase?" I asked, nearly shouting again. "Let's go!"

"There must be an elevator, right?" wondered Mae hopefully. "Please tell us we don't have to climb again."

The Golden Lion shook her head. Just before Paris fell to the Nazis, she said, French Resistance fighters cut the cables that operated the elevator. "If the Germans want to reach the top, they have to climb all the steps."

She beamed at her French friend. "But thank goodness we have the Parisian Light! She can transform us to fly like birds! It's the best way to go!"

The Parisian Light smiled smugly at Akiko.

"It's not exactly the *best*," Akiko said, just loud enough for Mae and me to hear. "Teleporting is still the best. But this will have to do."

Thirty-Four

MINUTES LATER, WE REACHED THE TOP. THE Parisian Light made sure to quickly transform Akiko, Mae, and me back into our human selves. But at the sound of something hitting part of the Eiffel Tower below us, she and the Golden Lion remained in their tiny bird forms. It was hard to hear—up so high, the wind blew loud in our ears—but I understood them to say they wanted to check out what was happening with the Metallic Falcon and report back. We watched them fly away.

Looking over the platform railing felt like peering down from a cloud. The air around us hummed louder than ever with Nazi aircraft. I spotted dive-bombers as well as fighter planes. And looking far below us at the city streets, I could see tanks and trucks. The Germans seemed to be readying for a big battle.

"There he is," said Mae, pointing down below us as the Metallic Falcon swooped low over the green parkland where our plane had landed. He reminded me of an enormous, terrifying gargoyle. Catching sight of his metal beak glinting sharp and dangerous in the sun, I had to step away.

When I turned around, I could hardly believe what my eyes landed on.

"Soldiers," I squeaked, grabbing Akiko's shoulder. "Right here! On the platform!"

Akiko and Mae saw them now. We dropped to the ground and tried to make a plan. There were two of them, and they both seemed to be napping in chairs in the opposite corner. I knew the noisy wind kept them from hearing us, but what if they noticed us staring at them? One of the soldiers leaned back in his chair, and I worried that a strong gust would blow him over—and wake them both up!

"Let's find Zenobia and get out of here," urged Mae, "before they even realize we're here."

We looked around, frantic to find any sign of the superheroes. There was a staircase above us that spiraled like a curly noodle. Was she up there? Would we have to climb another set of stairs? I leaned back against a wooden wall and tried to think as a powerful gust lifted my curls in all directions.

Akiko and Mae pushed their hair out of their eyes too. But then, over the noisy wind, the droning of the German planes, and the occasional boom of the Metallic Falcon's rage, we heard something.

"What is that?" Akiko exclaimed, putting a hand to the wall.

"Voices!" said Mae with a gasp. They both ran their hands along the wood, as if feeling for sound vibrations. "There's someone inside this room! Josie! Akiko! I think we've found them!"

But as we searched for a doorway, the wind howled louder than ever. And just as I feared, it toppled one of the sleeping guards from his chair. He scrambled to his feet in alarm. It woke his partner, too, who immediately spotted us and began yelling in angry German.

"Act like tourists!" I shouted. "Show them we're no threat!"

We put our hands up, indicating we meant no harm. Mae began telling them something about coming in peace, and I couldn't help but plaster what I hoped was a friendly smile on my face. But Akiko was the real hero.

"Chocolate! No need to get upset," she said calmly, reaching into her bag and pulling out two candy bars. "You can have our chocolate bars!"

"I can't believe it," I whispered, though I knew Akiko could hear me. "How many of those things do you have in there?"

Akiko inched toward the angry soldiers, her hands extending the chocolate bars. It was like she was approaching a lost dog, coaxing it to do her bidding.

"Listen, you two," she said quietly. "I'll give them the candy." It took me a moment to realize she was talking to Mae and me, not to the flustered Nazis. "But you two need to get over here and take care of them."

"What?" whispered Mae. "What are you talking about? I can't knock out a Nazi!"

"Yes you can," said Akiko, keeping her face calm as she took the final steps toward the soldiers. "Just like Noor Khan and Hopscotch showed us. You're going to have to get over here and flip them. Take them out."

I sized up the two soldiers, trying to guess how much they weighed. Could I really flip one of them over my shoulder?

"She's right, Mae," I whispered, slowly stepping in line with Akiko and trying to make my face look happy and not as terrified as I was feeling. "I'll take the one on the right. You take the one on the left. Once they're distracted with the candy bars, that's when we move. Got it?"

Mae said nothing, but she scooted beside me and gave a friendly-ish nod to the soldiers. "Chocolate," she said stiffly. "Yum?"

When Akiko reached them, the soldier on the left took the chocolate bar from her hand and began unwrapping it. After a few hungry bites, he let out a relaxed chuckle. They probably figured three kids posed no threat to their safety. Especially three scrawny, windblown girls.

"Whoops," said Akiko with a dramatic wave of her hands. "I dropped the other chocolate bar."

This was our signal to act. As the second soldier bent to pick up his bar, Mae and I swept in front of them. Recalling the steps Noor and Hopscotch had shown us, I grabbed one soldier by the arm, spun around, and pulled with all my might. His body flipped over my back and shoulder, then hit the metal floor with a heavy thud. By the way Akiko was cheering, it sounded as if Mae was trying the same thing.

"You've done it! Both of you!" shouted Akiko, pulling a length of rope from out of her bag. "Do you think this will hold them?"

"No need for that," came another voice. "Let them scurry away like a couple of rats."

The Parisian Light and the Golden Lion were back! They hovered near the railing, their jet pack and flapping wings helping them balance in the wind. Before Akiko had a chance to start tying the soldiers together, the Parisian Light snapped her fingers. In a flash, the Nazis transformed into a couple of beady-eyed, long-tailed rats. They scampered off down the staircase with high-pitched screeches.

"Thank you!" gasped Mae, her chest heaving as she tried to catch her breath. "That was a little too close."

"Come on," urged Akiko, racing toward the apartment door. "These goons were guarding Gustave's secret. Let's get in there!"

She tried the knob, but the door was locked.

"Mae!" she exclaimed. "Remember when you picked that lock in San Francisco? We need to use your spy skills again."

Mae wasted no time. Slipping a hairpin from one of her curls, she inserted it into the doorknob. With a few flicks and turns, we heard the sound we needed. The *click* of the lock slipping.

"You know, the Golden Lion has superstrength just like you, Josie," said the Parisian Light with a bouncy laugh. "She could have opened that door with her pinkie."

"Why didn't you tell us?" asked Akiko, who was no longer hiding her irritation.

"Because," said the Golden Lion, looking amused, "it's so much more interesting to see all the things you three can do *without* superpowers!"

Thirty - Five

$\mathcal{M}$AE PUSHED OPEN THE DOOR, AND WE raced inside the apartment.

The room was brightly lit, with sunshine streaming in through the windows. A woman at the center of it all jumped to her feet when she noticed us. She was tall and square shouldered, and her eyes reminded me of Mrs. B's.

"Dolores," a man called to her, "what do they want?"

She stepped toward us, looking alarmed. I remembered Mrs. B telling us her sister's name was Dolores. But to me, there was only one thing to call her.

"Zenobia," I whispered. "Is it really you?"

"We've come to the rescue," said Mae, sounding a little awestruck.

"To rescue you, as well as all the others," added Akiko, looking around us.

From the sofas and chairs, people jumped to their feet. There were men and women, short and tall. They seemed to be everywhere—spilling toward us from the back of the room, lining the round walls of the apartment, and rising from tables and benches throughout. How many were here? Fifty? Sixty? More?

"Who are you?" she asked urgently. "How can we trust you? The Metallic Falcon, the Hisser, Side-Splitter—so many have tried to trick us already."

I turned to Akiko and pointed frantically at her bag.

"The moonstone," I whispered. "Show her, Akiko!"

Akiko seemed to suddenly remember the most important thing we'd tucked away in her Hauntima pouch: the moonstone ring. It was an exact match to the one we'd already returned to Mrs. B, along with Astra's moonstone collar. The Palomino and Zenobia were the daughters of the Masked Moonflower, who drew her power from the moon. And she'd passed along special powers to her children in the form of these moonstones.

"Here it is," Akiko said, nearly panting as she opened the small box. "This ring. It's yours!"

Zenobia stared at the glimmering moonstone that rested

in Akiko's outstretched palm. It seemed to pulse with life.

"We work with Room Twelve," Mae said, trying to explain. "With Mrs. B and Astra. They've become weakened by this . . . this . . . whatever you call it—"

"This power that's drained all of you," interrupted Akiko. "It stripped away our power too. You wouldn't know it from looking at us—three powerless kids. But Josie, Mae, and I are the Infinity Trinity. We thought we'd be able to use our superpowers to get you out of here."

"But instead we've had to come like this. We couldn't ask your sister and Astra to fight," I said. "The Metallic Falcon is too dangerous. They'd be risking their lives."

She stood in silence, staring at us.

"And you?" asked Zenobia. "Without your superpowers, aren't you putting your own lives at risk?"

None of us spoke. What good were we now? What could we possibly do to take down a villain as powerful as the Metallic Falcon? A mix of anger and frustration churned inside me thinking about the loss of our powers.

Zenobia held the moonstone ring in both hands, studying the milky-white gem set in heavy gold. "Knowing what we're all up against, knowing that your powers are compromised . . ." She paused before looking back at us. "It means the world to me that you've come. That you've tried."

As she raised the moonstone ring—to the middle finger of her right hand—another hush fell over the room. I held my breath, and I heard Mae gasp beside me. Akiko's breathing seemed to catch too. We watched the ring slowly slide over her knuckle and then into place.

Immediately, an electrical charge sizzled through the whole apartment. The air seemed to crackle and spark, and a thrumming energy pulsed in my ears like a radio was suddenly plugged into a wall socket. The whole room came roaring back to life.

Bang!

All at once the floor beneath our feet shook. Had one of the Nazi planes struck the Eiffel Tower? Was the platform collapsing? Or was the Metallic Falcon turning his deadly attack here?

From the far side of the room came a murmur, and people began jumping aside and calling out. Something seemed to be wrong over there.

"What is it?" shouted a woman behind us. "What's happened?"

"There's a trunk!" someone answered. "It materialized out of nowhere!"

The crowd opened up to make room as two people—a man on the left, a woman on the right—lugged a heavy-looking steamer trunk forward and set it at Zenobia's feet. It was brown and rectangular, like any other trunk used for traveling. But something about it caught my eye.

"Those symbols. Right there, on the edge of the lid," I whispered, gawking at the familiar shapes I'd seen back in Philadelphia and San Francisco. "Akiko! Mae! This isn't just any steamer trunk.

"This trunk belongs to Mrs. B!"

Thirty-Six

"FINALLY," CAME A FAMILIAR VOICE, "WE'RE together again."

All heads turned to the doorway. Mrs. B and Astra were standing there, flanked by the ghostly forms of Nova, Hopscotch, and Hauntima. I felt panic bubble up inside me as I wished I could somehow protect them. In their weakened state, any sort of battle against the Metallic Falcon would be too much.

But before I could protest, Mae took my arm.

"It must be the moonstones," she whispered, unable to hide her excitement. "The moonstones are connecting them again—it's what brought them here."

Without another word, Mrs. B stepped to the center of the room. She extended her right arm, fist knotted tight, toward Zenobia. Time seemed to slow down as the sisters approached each other, Zenobia raising her fist in the same gesture and walking with her arm outstretched toward Mrs. B.

When the golden rings touched, the power of the moonstones erupted like a volcanic force. Blinding light radiated from their contact point, flowing up and out and all around the room. When I opened my eyes again, the apartment seemed bathed in a brighter light. Colors looked more vivid, and the faces of everyone around me appeared more alive than before.

"The sisters," came a shout. "They get their strength from each other!"

A golden mist, almost like a cloudy chrysalis, shrouded them. Then, as quickly as it appeared, it seemed to fall away. And they were transformed. Zenobia's ordinary clothes were replaced with tall gold boots and a shimmering golden cape emblazoned with a black Z. A sleek gold mask covered her eyes as she stared into her sister's face.

And where Mrs. B and Astra had stood a moment before, now two masked superheroes beamed in shimmering golden capes. The Palomino's candy-apple-red boots climbed to her knees. And Star reminded me of a powerful wolf.

"*Fantastique!*" whispered the Parisian Light.

"They're back!" hollered another voice, and the whole apartment roared in approval.

"We're *all* back," called the Palomino. And I could feel a new jolt of energy crackle throughout the room. It reminded me of dominoes, the way it seemed to pulse from one person to the next. Or maybe it was more like an ocean wave, crashing over us. I felt more alert and alive than I ever had in my life.

The Palomino quickly bent over the steamer trunk and fiddled with the lock. A moment later, I heard it click. And with a flick of her wrist, she flung the lid open. "What was taken from us is now returned. Together we can overcome the forces of evil!"

Again, sparks flew and a new buzzing filled my ears. It wasn't the frightening drone of the German planes. This sound was exhilarating, like a chorus of bumblebees. Full of promise. Potential. Hope. And through the golden glow that was radiating now from the trunk, almost like a bonfire, I could see the costumes that were waiting inside.

Superhero costumes.

Boom! Boom! Boom!

Outside the apartment, more explosions shook the ground. The Metallic Falcon must have sensed that something had changed at the top of the tower. That a shift had occurred. He was growing even more impatient in his search for the Infinity Trinity, and his terrible shouts and rants thundered even louder in our ears.

"Now we must act!" called Zenobia. "Claim your capes, masks, and boots, and unleash your strengths once again! The world needs you, more than ever before!"

One by one, the men and women of the room stepped to the trunk and seized their superhero costumes. My jaw dropped as I watched the line flow past us, as one after the next, heroes were reunited with their costumes. In a flash, they transformed.

At one point, the Stretcher approached to take his black costume from the Palomino's hands. His eyes were wet with tears. The Scarlet Singer, the Human Wrench, the Tiny Tumbler—so many superheroes I'd adored in comic books were ready to take to the skies again.

"Evil was winning," said the Ruby Hummingbird as she slipped into one ruby-red boot, then the other. "But no more. We fight for good. And we've had a lot of time to think about things. Now we act!"

In minutes, the apartment was teeming with caped heroes. And along with excited conversation, that same crackling energy surged and pulsed through the air with an even stronger intensity. It was as if a hurricane were building.

Even Nova, Hopscotch, and Hauntima seemed transformed. Stepping forward to join Star and the Palomino, they were no longer ghostlike and vapory. Now they looked sturdy and strong.

"We can win this together," said Nova. "Every one of us in the fight."

But Mae turned to Akiko and me, her expression desperate. "Everyone, it seems, except us."

Thirty-Seven

$\mathcal{T}$HE *RAT-A-TAT* OF NAZI PLANES AND THE crashing of the Metallic Falcon's latest attack snapped the whole room back to attention. Someone yelled something about getting moving, and suddenly the superheroes raced out the door and soared into the sky.

The three of us were left to watch from the sidelines.

"I am so grateful."

We turned to find the Palomino watching us. "Mae, Josie, Akiko, you kept pushing onward to find my sister, despite losing your own powers—and maybe even losing hope, too. But you never gave up."

"The world needed heroes," added Zenobia, "and you stepped forward. You tried to do what you could. And that is everything. The three of you were incredibly brave."

Akiko's breathing was hard. She pressed in closer to me, so our shoulders were touching. On the other side of me, Mae did the same thing. "We know bravery isn't just about big accomplishments," Mae whispered. "Bravery means you keep going, despite all the worries about failing."

"But thankfully," the Palomino said, adjusting her golden mask over her eyes, "you didn't fail."

I tried to keep a sob from escaping my throat. We had failed. The Infinity Trinity was no more. "We lost our powers," I said with a heavy shrug. "Something happened with the Metallic Falcon—it's like he knocked them out of us."

A fluttering noise from the balcony caught our attention. The Parisian Light and the Golden Lion hovered there, appearing torn between rushing off with the others to fight and sticking around to see what to do about Akiko, Mae, and me.

"Zenobia and the Palomino! We're so grateful you're back!" said the Golden Lion, gawking at the sight of them. "And Star too!"

"Finally we have a chance to defeat evil," cheered the

Parisian Light. "With so much power in the sky once again, we can't be stopped!"

Zenobia and the Palomino—she looked nothing like Mrs. B now—sounded tense as they talked about the battle that lay ahead for the superheroes. The Metallic Falcon's strength, the number of Nazi planes in the sky, the threat of attacks from all directions.

"What about the Infinity Trinity?" asked Akiko. "We want to be in this fight too."

The Palomino gently shook her head. "You have succeeded in your mission. However, the final battle is entirely too dangerous for superheroes as young as you," she said. "There was much discussion in Room Twelve after we lost contact with the Infinity Trinity. And we came to the conclusion that we have asked too much of you already."

Zenobia nodded in agreement as she gazed on the Parisian Light and the Golden Lion too. "It's not right to put you in such danger. After all, you're just children."

Just children?

Akiko coughed. I felt a tremor of outrage. With one eye, I caught a glimpse of the Golden Lion putting her hands on her hips defiantly, while the Parisian Light let out a *Pfft!* that blew her bangs straight up.

It wasn't too long ago that we were protecting them from danger!

"I know my Granny Crumpler would not like me pushing back against what a grown-up says," began Mae in her polite way. "But I have to speak up." She paused, taking a deep breath. "We are children, yes. But we've proven ourselves to the league of secret heroes again and again. Just because we're not adults like you all doesn't mean we can't help fight this war."

A look passed between the Palomino and Zenobia.

"We know you have much to offer," Zenobia began. "The fact that you've reached us here, at the top of the Eiffel Tower, is incredible. But we cannot ask you to battle a villain as sinister as the Metallic Falcon. Especially when he's bent on your destruction."

I shook my head. We'd come too far to sit this out.

"We've said it before: Every one of us brings something different to the fight," I said. "Akiko's clever thinking with her pouch and the way she uses fire. And Mae with her smarts when she reads minds and communicates with animals. They're remarkable—"

"And you too, Josie," interrupted the Golden Lion with a shake of her wings. "I saw the way you use your superstrength and telekinesis. You bring so much as well."

The Parisian Light joined with her, and they settled beside us.

"So yes, we are children. But we're more than *just*

children," I pushed. "We're smart and capable and brave like any other superhero. And more than anyone, we want to make sure that good triumphs over evil. Because we're the next to lead. We're the ones to inherit this world, for good or bad."

"And we want to make sure good triumphs," added Mae. "Just like it does in comic books."

Zenobia and the Palomino fell silent. Star stopped wagging his tail.

"All we need is to figure out how to get our costumes back," said Akiko, peering into the empty steamer trunk. "I don't understand why they aren't in there. Doesn't it make sense that our capes, masks, and boots would be inside? With all the others?"

The Parisian Light made a hiccuping sound.

"*Oui!* Why didn't you say something sooner?" she asked, then snapped her fingers.

Suddenly her arms overflowed with bright orange, vivid purple, and vibrant green. "We picked these up from the bridge, when the Metallic Falcon almost turned you into *fromage fondu*," she said. "Here you go."

"*Fromage fondu* is French for 'melted cheese,'" explained the Golden Lion. She gave us a friendly smile as she tried to catch one of Mae's purple boots before it fell. "The Parisian Light's matter manipulation comes in handy a lot. It's one of the best superpowers."

"Not really *the best*," started Akiko. "There's telep—"

"Thank you both," Mae said, beaming as she wrapped her arms around her violet costume. "I'm glad we can be there to help each other. As someone wise once told us, 'None of us is ever truly alone in the fight.' Let's get out there—now."

Thirty-Nine

*A*KIKO, MAE, AND I SWOOPED HIGHER IN the sky as we watched the Metallic Falcon plunge back to earth. The impact seemed to disturb not just the ground but the air as well, and the deafening crash made me plug my ears.

Dust and ash blew everywhere as we hovered above the city, trying to catch our breath. The blue Paris sky, which earlier had been filled with Nazi planes, was empty now. It was as if the Metallic Falcon pulled all the evil from the atmosphere as he tried to stop himself from falling.

Then a cheer erupted behind us.

"Look," whispered Mae. "I've never seen anything like it."

All around us, superheroes were soaring. Their capes rippled in the wind as they flew above us and below, some circling the sky as if running a victory lap. The Ruby Hummingbird turned flips in excitement, and the Stretcher pumped a black-gloved fist into the air triumphantly.

"Help," came a faint shout just beneath us. "Infinity Trinity! Help!"

As we swooped downward, it became clear who was calling. The Parisian Light was in distress. Her jet pack choked and sputtered as she tried to fly with the Golden Lion's body in her arms. The Lion hung as limp and lifeless as a doll.

"The Lion! Her strength is giving out," she gasped. "The bullets from the planes bounced right off her. But battling that awful tin bird—it strained her wings."

Mae asked if she could make it back to the Eiffel Tower. But the Parisian Light shook her head. From the sound of her jet pack, the distance was too far.

"I've got you," said Akiko, rushing to the Parisian Light's side. "We'll teleport. The Emerald Shield and Violet Vortex can meet us there. Don't worry."

A moment later, we heard a *Pop!* and they were gone.

Mae and I took off for the tower, leaving the rest of the superheroes to celebrate in the skies around Zenobia, the

Palomino, and Star. When we reached the top of the Eiffel Tower, the Golden Lion was lying on her side near the apartment door and trying to catch her breath.

We landed and raced closer to see what was wrong. Her wings were badly damaged, and feathers were missing in wide patches. From the corner of my eye, I saw Mae turn back toward the railing and call into the sky. She must have been summoning birds to flock to us and offer help.

"The Emerald Shield has healing powers," whispered Akiko in her not-so-quiet way. "She'll fix her up in no time."

I'd never seen anything like the Golden Lion's wings. The feathers were honey colored and as long as my hands. She'd folded her wings tight, so they seemed to tuck into each other along the whole length of her back—from her neck all the way to where her legs began. Even folded, though, I could tell how strong they were. And when I laid my hands on them, they felt muscular but at the same time weightless.

I squeezed my eyes shut and thought about how much she'd helped us. How important she was to the fight against evil. How much her best friend, the Parisian Light, needed her. How much the world needed her.

"Hey, Em!" croaked Akiko. "I think it's working!"

I opened my eyes and fell onto my backside, exhausted.

I could feel sweat beneath my mask as I adjusted it.

"Emerald Shield, is that you?" the Golden Lion asked groggily. "What happened? Is everyone okay?"

Suddenly we heard a fluttering of wings. I looked up just in time to see Mae in conversation with a row of birds that were now perched on the railing. Others hovered in the air just above us. There were tiny golden finches, fierce-looking golden eagles, noisy golden pheasants, and some others I couldn't identify. They seemed to be allowing Mae to take a few feathers before flapping off again.

"These should help repair her wings," Mae said at last, passing them to me. "Gifts from some friends."

Once I layered them into the bald patches, the Golden Lion got to her feet. She shook out her arms and legs and wings as if drying off from a shower. Then she turned to the three of us.

"Thank you, Infinity Trinity. I'm so grateful for the help."

"No," I said, looking from her to the Parisian Light. "We're the ones who are grateful. If you hadn't thought to grab our costumes off the bridge, we'd never have been able to fight the Metallic Falcon."

The Parisian Light nudged Akiko's shoulder.

"And if it weren't for you, I'd never have gotten the chance to teleport!" she exclaimed. "It really is the best way to get around."

"I told you!" croaked Akiko happily. "Hauntima's ghost! Finally somebody understands me!"

"Oui!" said the Parisian Light with a knowing wink to Mae and me. "I understand you perfectly, Orange Inferno. Perfectly!"

Forty

So, LET ME GET THIS RIGHT, AKIKO," MAE was saying. "You could have pulled a chocolate malted out of your bag the whole time?"

"And blueberry pie?" I wanted to know.

We were seated at a table inside Nova the Sunchaser's plane, which she'd reassembled from a sleek glider into a bulky transport plane. Akiko began explaining how she'd needed something to splash across the Nazi pilot's windshield during the battle near Big Ben. But I was having trouble concentrating. All I could think about was getting back to Philadelphia and sitting down at Gerda's Diner for my favorite meal.

"No need to debate the merits of milkshakes as weapons," announced Mrs. B, the gray waters of the English Channel spreading out far below us through the windows behind her. "We know you would probably prefer sipping one instead."

And from the back of the plane, two trays were passed up to us. The first held three tall glasses topped with whipped cream and cherries. We could tell which milkshake was which by their colors: Akiko took her egg cream, Mae held her chocolate malted, and I picked up my brown cow. When the second tray was set down, I closed my eyes and inhaled the delicious aroma of warm fruit. Three slices of pie were looking back up at us—apple, cherry, and blueberry.

"I wish we could give Aunt Willa and Aunt Janet pie and milkshakes too," said Mae as she gazed out the plane's window. "I wonder which flavors they'd pick."

Akiko and I crowded closer to Mae and peered through the glass. Mae's aunts were soaring in the sky off the right wing, keeping pace beside us in the shiny silver Texan we'd borrowed from the airfield as we flew back to London.

"Thank goodness they're all right," I said. "I'm glad you were able to give them back the things we found on the runway in Chicago."

We watched as Aunt Janet, wearing her round aviator's

goggles, gave us a thumbs-up. Aunt Willa waved, and her silky white scarf draped down her back.

"That scarf is like a cape," whispered Mae.

"And their goggles remind me of a mask," I added, spreading my fingers on the cold glass.

"Don't forget their tall boots," said Akiko. "They're like Nova's. And the Palomino's. They're like all of ours, really—"

"Like so many in the league of secret heroes," added Zenobia with a quiet smile. Her expression was cryptic, reminding me of a code that needed cracking.

"Are you telling us," said Mae, pausing for a beat or two as puzzle pieces in her mind clicked together, "that my aunts are part of Room Twelve?"

She slumped backward onto Akiko and me as the realization knocked the breath out of her lungs. Zenobia looked past us out the window, her expression proud as she studied Aunt Willa and Aunt Janet.

"As we said in San Francisco about Akiko's mother," explained Mrs. B, "the key element of our league of secret heroes is just that: secret. We look for the best, brightest, and bravest wherever we can find them. From Chicago airfields to San Francisco code rooms to Philadelphia computer basements. Even under the watchful eye of Fifinella in the middle of Texas."

At the mention of Fifinella, we turned and looked out

the left-side windows. Jane and Jackie were flying there, both wearing their leather jackets with the WASP patch over their hearts. I could picture the winged gremlin Fifinella in her tall red boots, and how it was painted on the sign welcoming all the pilots to Avenger Field.

The clattering of a dish caught my attention. Behind us, Astra was finishing off his pie and bumping the plate with his nose across the plane's floor. His tail wagged as he looked up at me, clearly as much a fan of pie as I was.

"As to what's ahead when we return," Mrs. B announced in her steady voice, "you can take comfort knowing that the spies in Chicago have been arrested. They will not pose a threat to anyone again—in Chicago or elsewhere."

I couldn't help but let out a sigh. I heard Akiko and Mae do the same.

"And Mae's grandmother has returned to Philadelphia to open another new library," Mrs. B went on. "So the three of you will be able to enjoy the last weeks of your summer vacation there before school starts."

Akiko and I grinned, and I was already thinking about going to the movies and playing Parcheesi with my little brothers and consuming as many pies and milkshakes as possible.

"What happens next?" I asked, turning to Mrs. B and Zenobia. "Do we go back to being just ordinary kids again?"

"You'll never be ordinary," answered Mrs. B, gently

shaking her head. "But until Room Twelve needs your services again, we hope you'll resume the simple pleasures of life. That's what Dolores and I plan to do."

Zenobia—I could never call her Dolores—took a sip of her milkshake and watched the three of us. "We're so grateful for your service. As we said goodbye to your new friends the Parisian Light and the Golden Lion, it occurred to me that I had been wrong. There is no such thing as 'just kids.'"

She set her glass down on the table, then paused as if collecting her thoughts.

"When the world needed heroes, each of you became one. You didn't just talk about it—you actually did something. You tried. And you showed such bravery," she said, her gaze moving from Akiko to me, then settling on Mae. "You faced your fears and you pushed past them.

"Your achievements in our league of secret heroes are a cause for celebration. And the Infinity Trinity's name now stands as an example to every one of us. But *especially kids.* Because, after all, you're our future. You're the reason we're in this fight."

My heart swelled at Zenobia's words. I looped one of my arms through Akiko's and the other through Mae's, knowing they must have felt just as proud. We did what we could for my dad and Mae's, for Akiko's brother, for everyone we loved. And while I was excited to get home and see Mam and my little brothers, my feet already itched to wear my green boots again. To feel my mask over my eyes and the wind rippling my cape.

"I hope we team up with the Parisian Light and the Golden Lion again," Akiko said. "And all the others."

"We're in Nova's plane," Mae reminded us. "Maybe she'll fly us all the way to Philadelphia."

"Nova, Hopscotch, Hauntima," I began. "And also the Stretcher, the Ruby Hummingbird. Maybe we can practice with them and sharpen some of our superpowers."

Akiko let out a series of quick sneezes.

Ah-choo! Ah-choo! Ah-choo!

Pulling a hankie out of her Hauntima bag, she blew her nose. Then she fidgeted for a few moments as if she had something on her mind.

"Mae, I meant to tell you," Akiko said. "You weren't half-bad flying the Texan to the Eiffel Tower."

"And you with the secret codes." Mae laughed. "You did all right."

"Don't forget flipping bad guys, computing calculations, and picking locks," I reminded them. "Even when we weren't flying around as the Infinity Trinity, we still had plenty of powers."

And that was the best feeling of all.

As sunlight glinted on Jane and Jackie's plane and Willa and Janet soared beside us on the other side, my heart was full. For too long we'd felt powerless. But now something replaced that feeling. Was it hope? Or confidence? Or maybe a sense of being part of something bigger than ourselves?

The league of secret heroes. I thought of my cousin Kay and Jean and the ENIAC Six, code crackers Elizebeth and Genevieve, the spy Noor Khan, and so many others we'd met in Room Twelve. They used their brains, their wits, their own special skills as best they could. And they showed Mae, Akiko, and me that we could too.

A grin took over my face as I sipped my milkshake. Mae and Akiko were starting up their back-and-forth banter, this time about what superpower was best for nighttime flying. I couldn't wait for what lay ahead for the three of us. Not everyone we'd meet would be wearing a cape, mask, and boots. But if we paid attention, I knew we'd be able to see the superhero inside.

AUTHOR'S NOTE

$\mathscr{M}$Y FAVORITE PART OF BEING A WRITER IS getting to dive deep into research. Gathering information for *Boots*, I wanted to learn more about the early female pilots who earned their flying licenses before and during World War II. At the time, women were not allowed to serve in the military. Critics believed women were too nervous for flight and not strong enough to handle big planes. But female pilots proved the doubters wrong.

As I began reading about the WASPs—the Women Airforce Service Pilots—they seemed like an organization rooted in the distant past. But I quickly realized that their legacy was still very much alive. I headed off to

Sweetwater, Texas, to attend one of their annual home-coming celebrations at the place where they'd trained during the war: Avenger Field. And while I was there, I was lucky enough to meet some of the pilots. Though they were in their nineties, these women were generous with their stories and their time. The experience gave me an incredible feeling of connection to WWII history—one I'll always treasure.

While *Cape*, *Mask*, and *Boots* are works of fiction meant to entertain, they're also meant to inspire. The characters of Josie, Mae, and Akiko—though fictitious—are in many ways everyday people just like you and me. They possess the potential to do good in the world, the same way we do. And they draw inspiration from the remarkable real-life heroines of WWII who worked so hard to fight back against evil. That's something all of us can do too. Here are some of the facts amid the fiction.

Willa Brown
Credit: Image courtesy of the Schomburg Center for Research in Black Culture,
Photographs and Prints Division, The New York Public Library.

Willa Brown

In 1934, when **Willa Brown** wanted to learn to fly, racial segregation prevented her from enrolling in classes with White students. She had been inspired by Bessie Coleman, who in 1921 had become the first African American woman and Native American woman to earn a pilot's license—though she'd had to go to France to do it. Willa began flying lessons at Chicago's first airport for African Americans, Harlem Field, on the southwest side of Chicago. After earning a mechanic's license, she went on to become the first Black woman in the United States to earn both a private pilot's license and a commercial pilot's license.

Deeply committed to racial and gender equality in flying, Willa joined with other Black pilots to draw more African Americans into aviation. With her husband, Cornelius Coffey, she ran a flight school and formed an organization to promote Black pilots serving in the military. Early in WWII, African Americans were limited to service jobs—as cooks, stewards, gravediggers. Through the hard work of Willa's flight school, the US government soon came to accept that Black pilots could be just as capable as Whites. She went on to train pilots to serve in WWII, including the famous Tuskegee Airmen, and was instrumental in helping to integrate African Americans into military service. Read more about Willa at the National Archives. (https://prologue.blogs.archives .gov/2019/10/22/the-maker-of-pilots-aviator-and-civil-rights -activist-willa-beatrice-brown/)

Janet Harmon
Credit: Image courtesy of the National Air and Space Museum,
Smithsonian Institution Archives.

Janet Harmon

As a girl, **Janet Harmon** was also inspired by Bessie, and by the idea of taking to the skies like a bird. In the 1930s, she saw a billboard reading "Birds learn to fly. Why can't you?" That did it—she signed up to take flying lessons. But when Janet came to class, she was the only woman. She'd already earned a nursing degree at college, so when her class needed a plane to practice with, Janet had money saved up and could help. She spent $600 on a bright red biplane with two open cockpits and shared it with fellow students. Always generous with her time and talent, Janet teamed up with Willa and other Black instructors to form a flying club, encouraging more African Americans to earn their pilot licenses.

In 1943, Janet applied to be part of the WASPs but was denied. Segregation in all aspects of the military and American society blocked her way. "I was refused," Janet wrote in her biography, *Soaring Above Setbacks*, "because of the color of my skin." Still wanting to serve her country, Janet read a newspaper article about a shortage of military nurses and decided to apply to the nurse corps. But again, she was rejected and told "the quota for colored nurses is filled." Finally, using all her savings, she flew to Tuskegee, Alabama, to take the flight test for her commercial pilot's license. After being denied the certificate because she was both Black and female, Janet returned to Chicago. Taking the test one more time, she finally was awarded her certificate, becoming the first African American woman to earn a commercial pilot's license. "There were so many things they said women couldn't do and Blacks couldn't do," she said in an interview in the *Chicago Tribune*. "Every defeat to me was a challenge." Listen to Janet's story here: https://siarchives.si.edu/blog/janet-harmon-bragg-female-aviator

**WASP pilots in their oversize training jumpsuits,
1943, Sweetwater, Texas**
Credit: Image courtesy of the TWU Libraries Woman's Collection,
Texas Woman's University, Denton, TX.

The WASPs

The **Women Airforce Service Pilots (WASP)** program was
established in 1943 to train female pilots to support the
US military. Their role included ferrying all kinds of aircraft across the country from factories to bases where they
were needed. With a goal of freeing up male pilots for combat, the WASPs also transported equipment and person-
nel, tested aircraft that had been repaired to ensure safety
before male pilots flew them again, trained other pilots,

and even towed targets for gunnery practice. While they were denied admittance, they trained and drilled as if they were part of the US military, flying all seventy-eight different types of army air force planes, from practice aircraft to high-powered pursuit planes to bombers.

WASPs spent thirty weeks in training, learning Morse code, weather science, physics, navigation using charts and maps, advanced math, first aid, and more. More than 25,000 women applied to be a WASP, but only 1,074 graduated from the program and earned their silver wings from founder Jacqueline "Jackie" Cochran. WASPs were proud of their wings, as well as the WASP mascot, Fifinella, which was drawn by Disney artists and traces its origins to author Roald Dahl's first children's book. In 1944, the WASP program was disbanded. It would be thirty more years before women were allowed to fly again for the US military. Learn more by visiting the National WASP WWII Museum in Sweetwater, Texas, or online at WASPmuseum.org. And explore the extensive WASP digital archive at Texas Woman's University. (https://twudigital.contentdm.oclc.org/digital/collection/p214coll2)

Jane Baessler at Avenger Field, wearing her flying jacket with the Fifinella logo. Jane saved the *LIFE* magazine that inspired her dreams of flying with the WASPs.
Credit: Photos courtesy of Jane Baessler Doyle's family.

WASP Pilot Jane Baessler

When **Mildred "Jane" Baessler Doyle** was a little girl in Grand Rapids, Michigan, the idea of flying captivated her. At eighteen, she earned her private pilot's license. But when she tried to continue flying at college, she was denied—women weren't allowed in the piloting classes. So she joined the Civil Air Patrol, a civilian aviation program, and kept up her skills. Soon after she read about women pilots in *LIFE* magazine, Jackie Cochran's telegram arrived asking her to join the WASP program at Avenger Field. Jane was ready. "My teachers tried to talk me out of it," Jane recalled when I visited her home in July 2018, when she was ninety-six years old. "But I told them I just want to fly."

Jane had a brother serving in the navy during the war, a sister in the Red Cross, and another relative fighting on the ground in Europe. As the baby of the family, Jane wondered what she could do to help. She believed flying was the answer, so she took off for Sweetwater, Texas. "The first time I got in that PT-19 with the helmet and the goggles," Jane recalled, "I thought, 'Oh boy! I'm a pilot now!'" Jane roomed with Odean "Deanie" Bishop Parrish during their WASP training in 1943 and '44, and they became lifelong friends. "Jane will climb in anything that flies," said Deanie's daughter, Nancy Parrish, in an interview with the *Detroit Free Press*. "I love that. It makes you go back in time and think, she must have been very spunky as a child." Watch an interview with Jane here: https://youtu.be/umUI4rJsr1ov

Air Force Lt. Col. Christina Hopper, veteran of Iraq
Credit: Photo courtesy of Tech Sgt. James Bolinger.

From Bessie Coleman to Willa Brown to Christina Hopper

Lt. Col. **Christina Hopper** was in college and part of an air force ROTC program when she first learned about barrier-breaking female pilots like the WASPs and Bessie Coleman. "Willa Brown impressed me with her courage to train African American men in a time when it was frowned upon," she told me in an interview, "and in a time when she wasn't allowed to serve in the military herself. I was very encouraged and felt like I was following in the legacy of amazing women." Lt. Col. Hopper made history when she flew an F-16—a single-seat, single-engine jet fighter—over Iraq in 2003, becoming the first African American female air force pilot to fly combat missions in a major war.

The early women pilots opened doors for aspiring fliers, Lt. Col. Hopper said, by refusing to be considered "less than" or incapable. "Their stories encouraged me when I felt like I was an outcast or like I did not fit in. I had to remind myself that I wasn't doing the things I was doing for my critics. I was doing it because it was what I was meant to do. When you know your purpose, it is easier to prevent others from discouraging you from your course."

An instructor in the air force reserve who trains pilots to fly supersonic fighter trainer jets, Lt. Col. Hopper is helping to raise the next generation of fliers. Her advice to girls who want to soar? Read books, attend camps, stay focused in school, study hard, and work on making the best grades possible. And get flying hours. While the number of women flying in the armed forces is still small, girls shouldn't be discouraged. "Don't allow others to tell you that you can't achieve your dreams," she advised. "The doors are wide open for you, so go for it!"

Major Katie (Higgins) Cook, Marine Corps pilot
and veteran of Afghanistan
Credit: Photograph by Balazs Gardi, courtesy of Major Cook.

WASPs Opened Up the Skies for Women

When US Marine Corps Major **Katie (Higgins) Cook** was young, she heard stories from both her grandfathers about their time as WWII pilots with the army air forces. And Katie's dad served as a navy pilot, so she had plenty of role models. But none of them were women. When she decided that she wanted to fly for the military too, she looked to the legacy begun at Avenger Field. "The WASPs carved the initial path," Katie told me in an interview, "and were a historical reference of use as proof that women belonged in the air." While WWII ended in 1945, it took almost fifty years before the US military would allow women like Katie to pilot fighter jets. "When I was on the Blue Angels as the first female pilot (in 2015), I could look back at the WASPs . . . and know they made so many sacrifices so that I could have these opportunities. I wanted to make them proud, live up to their legacy, and carve the path just a little bit further for those who came after me." Learn more about her at KatieAnnCook.com.

The *Chicago Tribune* from June 28, 1942

Spies in Chicago

"Operation Pastorius" was the name given to a Nazi spy
plot to bring the war to America's doorstep. It involved
sending eight German agents into American cities with
the intention of committing sabotage and spying. The plan
called for destroying railways, factories, and other key
industries and passing intelligence back to Germany. In
late June 1942, two German U-boats ferried two squads
of spies along the East Coast, landing them onto beaches
at Long Island, New York, and near Jacksonville, Florida.
Among the eight was Herbert Haupt, who had grown up on

Chicago's North Side and attended Lane Tech High School but had moved back to Germany. Days after the U-boat landing, Herbert reached his old neighborhood with treasonous plans to target a Chicago factory that made parts for the Norden Bombsight (which enabled US aircraft to drop bombs on the enemy with greater accuracy) and steal the blueprints. But before the spies could attack, one of the spies surrendered to the FBI. All eight spies were arrested, and six—including Herbert—were executed.

Double V Campaign

The Double V campaign was launched soon after WWII began, highlighting the fact that Black men and women were essentially fighting for victory in two wars: to defeat racism abroad and at home. While millions of Black men and women volunteered to serve their country, only a fraction were allowed to participate. Segregation prevented African American soldiers from serving beside Whites and confined them mostly to noncombat service roles, such as working in mess halls and on construction sites. But as the war progressed, African Americans began stepping into essential positions—as pilots, infantrymen, and officers, where they served with distinction. Yet when African American soldiers returned home from the war, they often were still denied basic freedoms such as sitting down to eat at restaurants where White soldiers dined. It wasn't until

1948, three years after WWII ended, that President Harry Truman outlawed segregation in the armed forces. Many African American veterans of WWII went on to become leaders in the modern Civil Rights Movement of the 1950s and '60s, fighting to put an end to segregation and discrimination in all aspects of American society. Learn more about African American contributions to WWII by watching this PBS documentary. (https://www.wqed.org/the-good-fight)

Gustave Eiffel's Secret Apartment

The Eiffel Tower was completed in 1889 and stands as a symbol of Paris, known around the world. Engineer and designer Gustave Eiffel enjoyed not only its fame, but also the private apartment he built for himself near the very top. Located on the third level, the secret hideaway was said to be "furnished in the simple style dear to scientists." He had many offers to rent the space but instead preferred to spend his time pursuing his own interests in the laboratory rooms he built there, running experiments on wind, astronomy, and physics, as well as entertaining other big thinkers. Thomas Edison was an early visitor and presented Gustave with one of his own inventions, a phonograph machine.

Spy Noor Khan

Noor Inayat Khan, who makes an appearance in *Mask* and is referred to in *Boots*, was a British agent fighting with the

French Resistance to defeat the Nazis. She parachuted into Occupied France in June 1943 as a radio operator under the code name "Madeleine." Though members of her spy network were arrested, Noor decided not to go home to London but rather to continue the dangerous work of transmitting coded messages out of France.

She was soon captured by the Nazi secret police, known as the Gestapo, and on Sept. 13, 1944, was executed at the Dachau concentration camp in Germany. Her WWII service is honored in London's Gordon Square, where a statue of her now stands. An engraving shares the last word she reportedly uttered before her death: *Liberté*. In English, it means "Freedom." Learn more about her at the Runnymede Air Forces Memorial. (https://www.cwgc.org/our-work/projects /noor-inayat-khan/visit-runnymede-memorial/)

RESOURCES

Books

Atwood, Kathryn J. *Women Heroes of World War II: 26 Stories of Espionage, Sabotage, Resistance, and Rescue.* Chicago: Chicago Review Press, 2011.

Gibson, Karen Bush. *Women Aviators: 26 Stories of Pioneer Flights, Daring Missions, and Record-setting Journeys.* Chicago: Chicago Review Press, 2013.

Harmon Bragg, Janet. With Marjorie M. Kriz. *Soaring Above Setbacks: The Autobiography of Janet Harmon Bragg, African American Aviator.* Washington: Smithsonian Institution Press, 1996.

Nathan, Amy. *Yankee Doodle Gals: Women Pilots of World War II.* Washington, DC: National Geographic Society, 2001.

Pearson, P. O'Connell. *Fly Girls: The Daring American Women Pilots Who Helped Win WWII.* New York: Simon & Schuster

Books for Young Readers, 2018.

Pyle, Ernie. *Ernie Pyle in England.* Ernie Pyle, 2016.

Takaki, Ronald. *Double Victory: A Multicultural History of America in World War II.* Boston: Little, Brown, 2000.

Videos

Collini, Sara. "Women Airforce Service Pilots (WASPs) of WWII." National Women's History Museum, April 23, 2019. https://www.womenshistory.org/exhibits/women-airforce-service-pilots-wasps-wwii.

Sobers, Kira M. "Janet Harmon Bragg: Female Aviator." Smithsonian Institution Archives, March 22, 2011. https://siarchives.si.edu/blog/janet-harmon-bragg-female-aviator.

Museums, Archives, and Websites

Grundhauser, Eric. "Secret Apartment on the Eiffel Tower." Atlas Obscura, August 23, 2006. https://www.atlasobscura.com/places/gustave-eiffel-s-secret-apartment.

Murphy, Rebecca. "See World War II through the Lens of an African American Soldier." Smithsonian Institution National Museum of American History, November 12, 2014. https://americanhistory.si.edu/blog/see-world-war-ii-through-lens-african-american-soldier.

Texas Woman's University. Women Airforce Service Pilots Official Archive. https://twu.edu/library/womans-collection/collections/women-airforce-service-pilots-official-archive/.

Tuskegee Airmen Inc. Willa Brown Biography. http://tuskegeeairmen.org/wp-content/uploads/Willa-Brown-Bio.pdf.

WASP Museum. The National WASP WWII Museum at Avenger Field in Sweetwater, Texas, celebrating the Women Airforce Service Pilots. WASPmuseum.org.

Wings Across America. Fly Girls of WWII Traveling WASP Exhibit. http://www.wingsacrossamerica.org/flygirls-exhibit.html.

Magazines and Newspapers

Grossman, Ron. "The Story of Chicago's Nazi Spy." *Chicago Tribune*, May 20, 2012. https://www.chicagotribune.com/ct-per-flash-germanspy-0520-20120520-story.html.

Lambertson, Giles. "The Other Harlem: In 1930s Chicago, at the Corner of 87th Street and Harlem Avenue, Cornelius Coffey Made Aviation History." *Smithsonian Institution's Air & Space Magazine*, March 2010. https://www.airspacemag.com/history-of-flight/the-other-harlem-5922057/.

Shamus, Kristen Jordan. "Michigan's Last Surviving WWII Fly Girl Recalls Her Time in the Sky, Blazing New Paths." *Detroit Free Press*, November 10, 2017. https://www.freep.com/story/news/2017/11/10/women-airforce-service-pilots-wasps-world-war-ii-michigan/837661001/.

ACKNOWLEDGMENTS

GRATEFUL THANKS TO THE LATE JANE Baessler Doyle and her family, especially Laurie Preston, who were so generous in talking with me in July 2018 so that I could learn more about Jane's time serving with the WASPs. Getting to see Jane's records and memorabilia was invaluable—and so exciting. As countless newspaper articles can attest, Jane was an openhearted woman with a wonderful spirit for adventure. She passed away on February 1, 2019, at age ninety-seven. Thanks also to US Air Force Lt. Col. Christina "Thumper" Hopper and US Marine Corps Major Katie Cook for letting me interview them for this book and helping me connect the dots between pilots like Willa Brown, Janet Harmon, Jane Doyle, and the WASPs and modern female pilots.

I appreciate the help I received from Ann Taub, lead archivist with the National WASP WWII Museum in Sweetwater, Texas, as well as Shelia Bickle, archives collection specialist and WASP expert with the Woman's Collection at Texas Woman's University in Denton, Texas. Thanks also to Hannah Byrne with the Institutional History Division of the Smithsonian Institution Archives for help with primary source material about Janet Harmon. And special thanks to fabulous Chicago Public Library librarian Lina Armstrong, as well as the amazing Jamelle St. Clair, a Chicago school librarian, for reading early drafts and offering crucial suggestions. Sincere thanks also go out to eagle-eyed reader Christina Hoover Moorehead and to my husband and most trusted critic, Naoum Issa.

And I am especially grateful to my editor, Alyson Heller, illustrator Patrick Spaziante, and the whole Aladdin team: Laura DiSiena, Alissa Nigro, Lauren Carr, Elizabeth Mims, Sara Berko, as well as the talented Elan Harris and Kelsey Eng.

ABOUT THE AUTHOR

*K*ATE HANNIGAN LOVES DIGGING UP remarkable people from history and sharing their stories for young readers. Honors for *Cape*, Book 1 in The League of Secret Heroes, include the 2020 Oklahoma Book Award in the Young Adult category, a Parents' Choice Foundation Recommended Award, and inclusion on the Illinois READS 2020 state reading list. Her historical mystery, *The Detective's Assistant*, about America's first woman detective, won the Golden Kite Award for middle-grade and was a California Young Reader Medal nominee. And her picture book biography, *A Lady Has the Floor*, was named a Junior Library Guild Selection.

Kate's superpower seems to be parallel parking, but if she could choose, it would be teleportation. She lives in Chicago with her husband, three kids, and two enthusiastic dogs. For curriculum connections and more information, visit her online at KateHannigan.com